D0369436

OPiNiONS AND OPOSSUMS
Ann Braden
ISBN: 978-1-9848-1609-2
Trim: 5 ½ x 8 ¼
On Sale: May 2, 2023
Ages 10 up * Grades 5 up
176 pages
$17.99 USA / $24.49 CAN

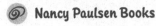 Nancy Paulsen Books

ALSO BY ANN BRADEN

The Benefits of Being an Octopus
Flight of the Puffin

OPINIONS
— AND —
OPOSSUMS

Ann Braden

Nancy Paulsen Books

NANCY PAULSEN BOOKS
An imprint of Penguin Random House LLC, New York

First published in the United States of America by Nancy Paulsen Books,
an imprint of Penguin Random House LLC, 2023

Copyright © 2023 by Ann Braden

Nancy Paulsen Books & colophon are trademarks of Penguin Random House LLC.
Penguin Books & colophon are registered trademarks of Penguin Books Limited.

Visit us online at penguinrandomhouse.com.

Library of Congress Cataloging-in-Publication Data is available.

Book manufactured in Canada

ISBN 9781984816092

1 3 5 7 9 10 8 6 4 2

FRI

Edited by Nancy Paulsen
Design by Marikka Tamura
Text set in Charter ITC Pro

For Dan,
the best partner ever.

How lucky I am that we get to sit next to each other on this ride
of life, thinking big thoughts, asking big questions,
and imagining the big, exciting lives of shopping carts.

In memory of my grandmother Jane Gracy Bedichek

LOTS OF KIDS HAVE TO GET BRACES, BUT NOT EVERYONE needs them because their adult canine teeth won't descend from the roof of their mouth. Weird, right? Just be glad you weren't there a few weeks ago when they excavated mine like I was a human archeological site. And it doesn't help that the neighbor who brings me to all my orthodontist appointments is always siting in the waiting room reading *Archeology Today* when I come out.

Today as my orthodontist tightened my braces, he joked that I was probably extra sweet since my sharpest teeth were buried so deep. I just nodded. It's not like I could say anything with all that equipment in my mouth anyway.

I didn't have anything to say as we drove home either. My mom was so relieved when Gracy, the neighbor lady, agreed to bring me to these appointments since my mom can't take time off from work. But it's awkward. Gracy tried starting conversations at the beginning. *"How's school?"* *"Fine."* *"What's your favorite subject?"* *"Lunch."* We didn't get much further since I was pretty sure there's not much someone around seventy has in common with a twelve-year-old kid. Now we mostly drive in silence.

Until this afternoon when Gracy screams: "Opossum!"

She slams on the brakes, and immediately the guy behind us starts honking. But instead of driving forward, Gracy turns off the engine and actually gets out. In the middle of the road!

"What are you doing?!" I call after her.

She says something, but I can't hear because of the honking. She pops the trunk and starts rummaging around. What could she possibly be doing? Maybe my mom shouldn't have been so eager to hand me to the first warm body with a car she found. I sink down into the seat so no one can see me.

But then Gracy opens my passenger door. She's wearing thick blue rubber gloves and points to something lying in the road.

"An opossum," she says. "We've got to save it."

What reality is this? I peer over the dashboard at the opossum lying in front of us. "Isn't it dead?"

"Probably just frightened into a state of shock." Gracy hands me a pair of gloves. "Agnes, if you help, we can move it to the edge of the road so it stays safe. There might be babies in the pouch."

"They have a pouch?" I say.

"Yes, they're our continent's only marsupials. Let's check."

I glance back at the line of cars forming behind us and the guy still honking his brains out. Everyone will see me if I get out of this car. I can't.

But what if there are babies in the opossum's pouch, and it's *my* fault they don't make it?

I pull on the gloves that Gracy hands me and join her beside the motionless opossum.

My breath catches in my throat as she gently opens the opossum's pouch to reveal what look like a dozen tiny, squirming babies. And I wanted to keep sitting in the car!

I squat down, and together Gracy and I carefully pick up the mama opossum's stiff body and start moving her toward the side of the road.

The guy behind us sticks his head out the window and yells, "Gross!"

That's probably what I'd have said a minute ago, too, but even though this opossum smells like a dumpster full of rotten trash, all I can picture are those babies. Do they deserve to be called gross?

We set the mama's body down away from the road, under some bushes at the edge of the woods.

"Do you think she really might still be alive?"

Gracy nods. "Opossums have evolved to 'play dead' when threatened since most animals won't eat one that's already dead. But this instinct isn't great if your predator is a line of traffic ready to run you over. Can you wait here while I move our car out of the way?"

I nod and study the mama opossum. Her teeth are bared, and they look super sharp.

Once Gracy's car is parked on the shoulder, the angry guy takes off, still yelling as he goes.

But Gracy doesn't seem bothered. She simply takes the gloves back from me. "I always keep supplies in my trunk for situations like this."

Really? Who is this woman? Maybe I should be talking to her after all.

I watch her as she calmly puts everything back in the trunk. "Why doesn't the opossum know to not cross such a busy street?"

Gracy gestures at an apple core on the edge of the road. "Part of the reason they've been a successful species for nearly sixty million years is because they follow the smell of food."

"Even if it means crossing a road with cars?"

Gracy shrugs. "Cars have only been around for a hundred years, and evolution is a slow process. The opossum certainly isn't the only animal that does what it's done for years, even if it doesn't make sense."

I picture what could have happened if Gracy hadn't stopped. How ridiculously unfair. All the opossum wanted to do was eat the apple someone must have thrown out their window.

I kick the apple core as far as I can into the woods. If anyone should be angry, it's the opossum. Is it her fault she did what millions of years of ancestors have done? And look what almost happened.

Gracy and I stay, watching the opossum from the car, until finally, she stirs, stands up, and walks into the woods, taking her babies with her.

Chapter 2

WHEN MY MOM GETS HOME FROM HER JOB AT THE BANK, I'm at the kitchen table looking at opossums on my phone. I never gave them a second thought before, but now I can't get them out of my head.

"Did you know that an adult opossum can eat five thousand ticks a year?" I say.

"That's a lot of ticks," my mom says as she drops her purse on the counter and starts going through the mail. "How was the orthodontist?"

"Fine." At least the appointment was. I don't have a word to describe what happened afterward.

My mom tugs off her stockings as she always does the minute she comes in the door. My mom hates stockings, but Mr. Adams, her boss, likes his female employees to wear skirts and stockings. It's not a written rule or anything, but my mom says that doesn't matter. So guess what she wears every day? Tight, itchy, sliding down stockings.

"There it is!" my mom says, pulling an envelope from the

mail pile. "I didn't want to miss it because we've got to fill this out and drop it off at church this weekend."

"What is it?"

"Now that you're twelve, we can sign you up for confirmation classes."

"What?! Do I have to?" I didn't have the best experience at Sunday school a few years ago when I made the mistake of asking what original sin was. I learned that 1) I should *totally* have known the answer already, and 2) Everything bad was Eve's fault from when she bit into that apple in the Garden of Eden. And to think I'd been excited that we were finally talking about a Bible story with a girl. Good times. I didn't ask another question in that class.

Plus, it bothers me that everyone at church is positive there's a heaven, and while I want there to be one, I'm not sure. I can't count the number of times someone's told me my dad is in a better place. Maybe that made them feel good, but I'd sure prefer if he was here. I wish I could even remember him, but I was too young when he died.

"Sorry," my mom says as she starts to fill out the form. "It's nonnegotiable. Not with your grandmother counting on you to be confirmed as a full member of the church . . ."

My grandmother—also named Agnes after St. Agnes—is super religious. But Florida is a long way from Connecticut. I start to say that, but my mom is still talking.

"And certainly not with Mr. Adams being president of the church board and talking for years about their membership targets." She finishes the form and tucks it in an envelope.

"Maybe we can't give much to the annual fund, but we can give him one more church member for his charts."

Rick Adams, president of the church board of trustees and president of the First Whitefield Savings and Loan bank where my mom works, has way too much control over our lives.

"Do we really have to care about his charts?" I ask.

My mom starts doing the dishes. "We do if I want to get promoted, and considering how much your braces are costing . . ."

"Yeah, I know," I say. "The promotion isn't optional."

I head to my room wondering why my mom insists on dragging me to church every Sunday (wearing stockings for the sixth day of the week!) when I'm not even sure *she* likes going. Not to mention, what was she thinking naming me after her super-religious mother?

Perhaps that opossum isn't the only one stuck in the middle of the road.

▲●■

In my room I look for my writing notebook before I realize it's my best friend Mo's turn with it. We do a lot of cowriting. Making up stories together is our thing. Specifically, stories about shopping carts. Basically, whenever we see an abandoned shopping cart, we write a story from the shopping cart's perspective. We've been writing them since fifth grade, and now we have three notebooks full of stories. *Shopping Cart Stories*, *More Shopping Cart Stories*, and *The Continuation of Shopping Cart Stories*.

But now I have a new inspiration—what about writing from

an opossum's point of view? What would that mother have said today if she could talk? *"Who are you calling gross? Are you carrying a whole bunch of babies around in your pouch? Have some respect!"*

I find another notebook, lie down on my stomach on my bed, and start writing.

THE OPINION OF AN OPOSSUM

Let me tell you how much I hate cars. We opossums have lots of jokes about them . . .

"Why did the opossum cross the road?"

"She didn't. She was smooshed before reaching the other side!"

And yeah, I'm sure it doesn't seem so smart to play dead in the middle of the street. Well, it's not my fault. I've been playing dead in the face of danger for sixty million years. Do you know how long cars have been around? About a hundred years. Do you know how much bigger sixty million is than a measly hundred? A lot. And do you know how hard it is to break a habit? Let's take for example a habit that human beings are quite used to— DRIVING CARS.

Now, most of the people who drive cars know that it's bad for the environment. But do they stop? No. Because they need to get to the grocery store.

So don't you be judging the opossum that walks to the edge of the road to eat that apple core.

Chapter 3

THE NEXT DAY AT SCHOOL, I TAKE A SEAT AT OUR TABLE in the corner of the cafeteria as Mo lays out the food his mom packed for him. Leftover baked ziti, carrot sticks, sour cream and onion potato chips, and a thinly sliced apple. Mo's right that apples taste better like that, but my mom says she doesn't have the time to cut my apples that way, plus she says it all goes to the same place anyway.

"So, what's this confirmation class thing you texted me about?" Mo says, starting in on the chips.

"Basically, we've got eight weeks to study and prove we're religious enough to officially become church members."

"Or else, what? If you can't prove it, do they send you off on your own iceberg?"

I smile. *"To float off into the frozen fog of the arctic . . ."*

"Like a peaceful icy cowboy," Mo finishes. That's one of our favorite lines. It's from a story about the shopping cart we found chained to a bin of ice outside a gas station.

"This is why I feel so lucky to have zero/negative zero

faith," Mo says. He always says that his mom's nonobservant Jewishness and his dad's lapsed Catholicism canceled each other out in a massive matter/antimatter collision. I've asked him which is the matter and which is the antimatter, but he just says, "The antimatter is the other one." And he calls it zero/negative zero because he can.

I picture the girls who I know will be in confirmation class, too—like our classmate Miranda. She's the daughter of my mom's boss, Rick Adams, so that's a done deal. Even though we're not friends, she always invites me to her birthday parties because it's the "Christian thing to do." Not like I enjoy having to go. Most of her friends spend the party fake smiling at me and then making fun of me as soon as they think I can't hear. It's easier at school, where they pretend I don't exist, but of course my mom wouldn't let me say no to that invitation. Just like how she won't let me get out of this class.

"Well, I hope the class isn't too terrible," Mo says. "You know people can be jerks."

"They sure can be. Can you believe that guy who yelled out of his car window?" I blurt out. "Who does that?"

"You're still thinking about that opossum hater?" Mo shakes his head. "Don't let yourself care about opopinions."

Opopinions is Mo's trademark word for Other People's Opinions. He should also trademark his ability to not actually care about them.

"What if they're opopinions about an opossum who can't stand up for herself because she's paralyzed in fear in the middle of the road?" I say.

"Opopinions about an opossum . . ." Mo repeats, and he must like the sound of it because he keeps saying it over and over.

"I'm being serious," I cut in.

"I'm sorry," he says as we both get up to head back to class. "I just don't think you need to get so worked up about it."

Not much bothers Mo. He's nearly a foot taller than he was last year but still wears the same sweatpants even though they end right below his knees. Actually, there is *one* thing that bothers him. Our school is kind of sports obsessed, and the basketball coach wants him to play. The coach even called his parents, and now they're bugging him to attend basketball camp this summer.

We dump our trash, and when we pass the bulletin board, Mo puts his arm out to stop me, just like my mom in the car when she slams on the brakes.

There's a new flyer announcing the town newspaper's annual student writing contest.

Mo grips my arm. "We're finally old enough. We've got to enter! Should we start working on a new shopping cart story after school?"

I shake my head and start walking toward our lockers. "Haven't we sort of exhausted the topic? How about we write something new from . . . an opossum's perspective?"

"But the judges will love our shopping cart stories!" Mo insists.

"I thought we weren't supposed to care about opopinions,"

I say. "Even from judges. And I think opossums might have a lot to say."

"But we always write shopping cart stories, and the next one is bound to be contest worthy."

I think of Gracy. Just because things have been done one way before doesn't mean it's the right way.

"What if a shopping cart runs into an opossum?"

"Mo," I interrupt.

"What?"

I swallow. "I don't want to do it."

Mo's mouth drops open. "No way. We are not going to NOT do it. You just need some inspiration. Let's go to the old park again for today's shopping cart hunting. We've found some great ones there."

I don't want to go shopping cart hunting. I want to go home and work on *The Opinion of an Opossum*. But I can't say no to Mo. Not when he cares about something this much.

"Fine." I sigh. "I'll go."

Chapter 4

WE GET OFF MY BUS THREE STOPS LATER THAN NORMAL but on a street that's nearly identical to mine where the houses are just as small and smushed together.

Mo starts walking down the sidewalk sideways. Actually, *leaping* down the sidewalk sideways.

"What are you doing?"

"We're hunting. I'm channeling my inner caveman."

I try to mimic one of his sideways leaps.

"There's no harder prey than a metal shopping cart," he tells me.

I do another small sideways leap. "You really think this is how cavemen hunted? I'm thinking it's more like how they walked when the ground was actually lava."

Just then, someone walks out of their door and goes to their mailbox. I start walking normally, but Mo doesn't stop. The guy stares. Mo doesn't ever seem to care, and I follow him down a dead-end street into the park.

There's an old playground here that no kids ever seem to

come to, probably because their parents prefer the newly renovated park on the other side of town where you don't have to fend off splinters.

"Which way?" Mo asks. "To the ball field or to the history of Whitefield area? Or over the dangerous bouncy bridge?"

"History of Whitefield," I say.

Mo nods and takes off his shoes and socks before sideways leaping away. "Try it, Agnes! The feel of the grass is wonderful!" he exclaims.

"I like keeping my shoes on," I say.

Mo leaps past the World War II memorial, the Korean War monument, and the monument to the town's founders. He suddenly stops behind the clump of trees that's next to the square monument. At least that's what I've always called it in my head. It's a big square plaque in front of a stone wall in the shape of a square.

"FATE!" he yells. "It's FATE!!!"

What's he talking about? I hustle to catch up with him.

And there behind the trees, inside the square stone wall, is a shopping cart.

Mo dances around it. "It's like the shopping cart gods looked down and saw you were getting bored and decided to give you your very own story!"

"Huh?" I say. "Why is this my story?"

"Well, it's your territory."

My . . . I look at the square plaque that he's pointing at, and for the first time ever, I actually read it.

HISTORIC TOWN SHEEP PEN

There used to be sheep here? My eyes snap to his. "What do sheep have to do with me?"

"Because remember how all those St. Agnes cards your grandmother sends you *always* have sheep on them? So you must be connected somehow . . ." He looks at me, and his face changes. Like he can tell I am in no way about to go along with this.

"I am named after my grandmother," I say. "Not some stupid sheep. And maybe it's just random that the cards have sheep on them."

"Come on," he says. "I didn't mean that in a bad way. Sheep are nice and fuzzy. And can you imagine if they were still here messing up this perfect suburbia? I mean, they poop all over the ground."

"Yeah, but sheep just follow other sheep around," I say. "Who wants to be considered a brainless follower?"

Mo looks down, and his shoulders drop. "I'm sorry." He peeks up at me. "If you want, you can call me MoMo for the rest of the day."

"Never mind," I tell him. I look past him at the tiny square of grass inside the walls. Why didn't they make the walled-in area bigger? Would the sheep have complained? Would they have said *anything*?

But Mo is still full of ideas. "Our story could be about a shopping cart that wakes up here, with no memory of leaving the grocery store parking lot, but it's secret dream was always to escape, and so now it—

I cut him off. "Mo, I'm not writing about any shopping cart."
I look him right in the eye. "I just want to focus on my opossum
opinions. And opossums and sheep are completely different."

"But, Agnes . . ."

I shake my head. I am not a sheep.

—— Chapter 5 ——

AS SOON AS I GET HOME, I DIG OUT THE MOST RECENT cards my grandmother sent me. Okay, so they all have sheep on them, but I'm sure that's just a coincidence. I flip one of the cards over. I've never read the small print on the back before.

And right away, I read that the name Agnes comes from the Latin word for lamb. And that it means "chaste" or "pure." Awesome. Evidently, St. Agnes is the patron saint of girls and chastity. Because every girl wants to identify with a pure, white lamb, right?

I also learn that St. Agnes was born in the year 291 AD into a Christian family. She was beautiful (thank goodness, no one likes ugly lambs), and the governor's son wanted to marry her, but she refused because she was devoted to God.

So they dragged her through the street and beheaded her.

When she was about twelve or thirteen years old.

What does it mean when a religion tells you a girl's most saintly act was to die?

18

I swallow.

I blink.

Then I put the cards back where I found them.

Sometimes there's a reason you don't want to read the fine print.

▲●■

After dinner, my mom and I are doing the dishes and listening to a political podcast while I'm trying to forget my newly discovered connections to sheep. It helps that my mom could never admit to the rest of her family that she listens to this show. My extended family is all there's-one-way-to-think-and-you-definitely-don't-question-it, so this is our secret. Really, it's quite unsheeplike.

I'm almost done with the dishes when my phone starts buzzing.

"It's Mo," I say. Mo and I have discovered that while our parents are super strict about screen time in the evenings, they'll happily let us talk on the phone.

My mom nods to my phone. "Go ahead. I can finish up the rest."

"Hey," I say as I head to my room.

"Hey," he says. "Any chance you've changed your mind about the sheep shopping cart story?"

"No!" I flop down on my bed.

"But you said that—"

"I'm not a sheep, Mo. Sheep go along with stuff they don't believe in. Stupid, chaste sheep."

"Whoa. You don't have to yell," Mo says. "And did you just say 'chaste'? I don't even know what that means."

I get up from my bed so I can pace. "Forget it. It doesn't even matter."

Mo is quiet for a long time.

"I'm sorry I yelled," I finally say.

"That's okay. Just at least listen to this beginning." Mo starts reading:

"Steve the shopping cart stared out over the park and thought his big thoughts: How did I get here? Was I really born to carry stuff? He knew there had to be more to life than holding basketball-sized cantaloupes. And even though he was alone for the very first time, and even though he didn't like being by himself, he made a decision. He was never going back to the grocery store."

"That's pretty good, Mo, but I'm not in the mood right now."

After I hang up, I pick up the confirmation class brochure on my desk. On the back is a quote from the Bible verse about the Lord being my shepherd.

I drop the brochure back on my desk.

What is it with me and sheep right now anyway?

THE OPINION OF AN OPOSSUM

Playing dead isn't really playing. What do you do when you encounter danger? Sometimes I growl and run, but when it's really intense, I faint. And I hear I'm not very pleasant then. I kinda drool and stink, and green mucus oozes from my butt. Fun times, right? I should get the Most Convincing Decaying Animal award.

But hey, it usually works! It doesn't matter how gross and embarrassing it is. Because no coyote wants to eat anything as smelly as me after I've gone down. So, an hour or so later (ASSUMING A CAR HASN'T RUN OVER ME), I pick myself up again and walk away, my dignity fully intact.

Like a real-life miracle.

Chapter 6

"I KNOW THIS ISN'T WHAT YOU'D CHOOSE TO DO ON YOUR Wednesday nights, but you and me, we're a team," my mom says as she drives me to confirmation class.

"Thank you," she says as she pulls in front of the church.

I nod because I get it. I get that we need that promotion, and I get that Rick Adams is the kind of boss where this stuff matters, and I get that we're a team, and maybe I'm not old enough to earn real money yet, so I can do this to help instead.

But it doesn't feel good just going along with stuff I'm not okay with. And I can't help thinking about sheep.

▲●■

When I get to the "pastor's parlor," the lights are all off, but then I see Miranda sitting primly in her chair like the perfect student that she is. Even though she's in the dark.

"Do you think we should turn on the lights?" I venture.

She looks at me, slightly horrified. "There's a sign that says to keep the lights off when the room isn't in use."

I pause. "Isn't it in use now?"

"But Pastor Paul isn't here yet."

I look at her. Then I eye the nearest lamp.

"I'm sure Pastor Paul will be here any minute," she says.

Fine. I take a seat.

Pastor Paul shows up just a few minutes later. "Ah, let there be light!" he says, flicking on the switch.

Tya, Miranda's bestie, arrives right after that, carrying her lacrosse stick and wearing a shirt that says "Black, Bold, and Beautiful." She gives Miranda a friendly poke with her lacrosse stick, saying something about lunch that makes her giggle. Tya sits at the popular table with Miranda, but she doesn't do the fake smiling thing like Miranda's other friends. Last year when I was in her English group, she was so funny telling us about her cat named Robot and how she swears he's an alien from another planet, that it made the whole group thing bearable.

The last and only other person to show up is Jaclyn. I'm surprised to see her here, as she spends most of her time at school in in-school suspension or rolling her eyes when our science teacher checks to see if she has her homework.

"So, just girls this year." Pastor Paul smiles as he settles into an armchair at the end of the table. "That's . . . different, but don't worry. I'm sure we can make it work."

I'm not sure what he means, but I bite my tongue. The only way I'm going to get through this class without screwing things up for my mom is if I keep my mouth shut.

"This class will set you on the path to being a servant of God and a dedicated member of our church," he says. "These eight weeks are an opportunity to ensure that each of you follows the example of the church's founding fathers to strengthen your faith and your bonds to this church, to leave the world a better place . . ."

Miranda is already taking notes like her life depends on it. I can't imagine it's easy living with her demanding father. Rick Adams has raised her by himself since her mom died of cancer when Miranda was little. Which is rough. I would know, right? Still, at least her family doesn't have to worry about money, and they do have a lot of help. Miranda's aunt lives next door and cooks them dinner every night, and they've always had a housekeeper, too.

"Now," Pastor Paul says, "before I pass out the special workbooks we'll use for this class, I want you to take a moment to look at each other. Make eye contact."

Miranda and Tya make eye contact, and I turn to Jaclyn, but she's keeping her eyes down on the table.

"The choice you'll be making to join the church as full members is a momentous one, and these are the people you're on this journey with," Pastor Paul says.

He gestures to a picture of a white-bearded God. "God is a constant source of strength, and you can be a source of strength for each other, too. Lean on each other when you have confusion or doubt." Pastor Paul closes his eyes, his hands clasped together. "I pray that each of you will embark on your own pathway to God."

Miranda and Tya have now closed their eyes, so I close mine, too. I try to picture what a pathway to God would look like. A staircase? A long accessible ramp? Glittering? Marble? I have no idea.

As Pastor Paul passes out the workbooks, he starts drawing on Bible stories to talk about the kind of church members we should be. Be willing to sacrifice like Abraham. Pray as often as Daniel. Obey the Lord better than Saul. Which makes no sense to me, because wasn't Saul the one who got in trouble for NOT killing every living thing in a city when God wanted complete revenge? But I don't ask, and no one else does either. Tya is flipping through the workbook. Jaclyn is tying knots in her hoodie drawstring. Miranda is nodding like she'd be fine slaughtering people if God asked her to.

My face must give my doubts away, though, because Pastor Paul pauses and smiles at me. "I know the Old Testament can be a bit intense, Agnes, but don't worry. We'll get to the New Testament soon enough."

I nod and try to slump lower in my chair.

Just like at school, Miranda is ready with the correct answer for every question Pastor Paul asks. But somehow, I can still see her sitting in the dark, feeling like she isn't allowed to turn on the lights.

When Pastor Paul leads us in prayer, "Our Father who art in heaven . . ." I mumble the words, but like always, I get twisted in knots about the beginning. Because it'd be nice to believe my actual dad is in heaven . . .

Miranda raises her hand again, but this time Pastor Paul hasn't asked a question.

"Yes, Miranda?"

"Sorry, Pastor Paul, but I was just thinking about what you said earlier. About how this is our opportunity to strengthen our bonds to the church, and how important it is for us to be able to rely on each other. And I was thinking that maybe we should first make sure we're all committed to the church."

Pastor Paul smiles like this most exemplary pupil is going to make his pastor heart burst. "How do you imagine doing that?"

"Maybe a pledge form or something?" Miranda says. "How about one that says we believe in God and are here to serve Him." She looks at me. "We could each sign it to show how dedicated we are."

My stomach drops away from me. Miranda says more things about how she can write it up and bring copies next week. Pastor Paul is practically leaping around with the excitement of it all.

What am I going to do? Do I actually believe in the God that punished Saul because he didn't kill absolutely everyone? Who got mad at Eve for taking a bite of an apple? Why was that such a big deal? Why did that story have to make God so focused on revenge?

None of this makes any sense to me, and I'm pretty sure this class, and these classmates, won't exactly help.

Chapter 7

MY MOM STICKS HER HEAD IN MY ROOM. "HAVE YOU done all your homework already?"

I nod, and she comes in and kisses the top of my head. She's already in her giant fleece bathrobe, and she smells like the clementines she's been eating as her "healthy dessert."

"Turn off your light soon, okay?" she says. "I'm heading to bed."

"I will."

"And your phone's downstairs already, right?"

I nod again.

"Hey, Mom?"

She stops in the doorway and turns back toward me. "Yeah?"

"What are you supposed to do when . . ." I pause. "When you're supposed to tell the truth, but telling the truth will cause problems?"

My mom's face freezes, and then she's right back next to me, sitting on my bed. "Is everything okay? You know you can always be honest with me, right? If you're doing something that you shouldn't be doing, I would rather—"

I cut her off. "It's not that kind of thing, Mom. It's confirmation class. Miranda is planning to bring in a form for us each to sign that says we believe in God, and I don't think I do."

Mom lets out a long breath. "I'm sorry." Then after a long moment, she says, "You'll have to sign it anyway."

"I figured."

"This is why we have white lies, right?" she tells me. "Like when Linda at work asks me if I like her new haircut, I always say yes. It doesn't matter if I don't."

I swallow. "Because we don't want to hurt feelings."

"Exactly," she says. She wraps her cozy, fleecy arm around me. "I know dealing with stuff like this can be tricky, Agnes. Just remember I have faith in you. I wouldn't want to be on anyone's team but yours."

"Me too, Mama." I burrow into her robe.

But as cozy as it is next to her, I can't help thinking that talking to Linda, who I think always looks great with any hairstyle, is different than signing a document that says you believe in God.

And how there must be *some* way to move forward in which I don't have to play dead.

THE OPINION OF AN OPOSSUM

Now, for the record, I hate playing dead. I mean who really wants to just drop to the ground and hope for the best?

But sometimes your only options are do what you want, OR SURVIVE. And I'm only here because my ancestors chose the second option.

But I would swear on all the stiff lifeless bodies of my ancestors that if I could change things so that survival did NOT require us to fully submit to those who just happen to be more powerful, I would.

Chapter 8

"I HAVE A QUESTION," I SAY. MO AND I ARE AT HIS HOUSE because: Better snacks. We have the house to ourselves since Mo's mom has taken his sister, Sadie, to her new dance class, so we've taken the liberty of opening a new box of all-butter coffee cake, cutting it down the middle, and loading two plates with our enormous portions.

Mo takes his first bite. He pauses, eyes closed, to savor all that butter. Then he opens his eyes. "Okay. Shoot."

"Do you believe in God?" I ask.

His eyes fly open. "Way to beat around the bush." He laughs.

"Do you?"

He takes another bite. "You know. Zero/negative zero faith."

"So you don't believe in anything?"

"I don't think so," he says. "But I don't really like thinking there's nothing out there either. Maybe we're all swimming in primordial chocolate soup, and the meaning of life is to stop and lick the flowers more."

"I'm serious, Mo."

"Well, I am too. I have no idea. Who really does? Who can say with certainty they know what's going on with all that stuff?"

"Lots of people."

"Well, good for them."

I take a bite of coffee cake. It is a pretty great feeling when a mouthful can taste this good and you still have most of a slice so big it barely fits on your plate. "And I'm supposed to."

"Supposed to what?" he says.

"Supposed to sign a paper at confirmation class that says I believe in God."

Mo nearly chokes on his cake. "What? Are you supposed to sign a paper that says that you've figured out what's inside a black hole while you're at it?"

I shake my head. "I think that'd be easier."

"Ha!" Mo smiles and looks off out the window. I'd bet anything Mo's remembering the story about the shopping cart who had dreams of being an astrophysicist and loved to stare up at the stars from the middle of the parking lot every night.

"*But a shopping cart is just one point in an enormous universe,*" I recite.

"*One point that can see all the other points and can finally feel at peace,*" he finishes.

"That was a good one," I say.

"I miss writing them with you," Mo says. "You're the one who was always good with the metaphors. It's not the same on my own."

"It's not forever," I tell him. "I need to work on my opossum stuff first. It's what's speaking to me now."

"Which you're not letting me read, by the way."

"It's too soon. But I told you it's about opossums. Isn't that enough?"

"Well, is it about more than just opossums?"

Is it? I stare at my plate. "Kind of."

Mo sighs. "Fine." He pokes me with his fork. "So, are you going to sign that paper at church?"

"I don't know. I want to believe in God, but I just can't get there. At least I'm not there yet."

"Well, then that's easy. Just don't sign the paper."

"But I can't *not* sign the paper. Miranda will flip out. Pastor Paul will flip out. Then I'll probably get kicked out of confirmation class and Miranda's dad will find out. He'll be 'disappointed,' and that means my mom won't get that promotion, and we won't be able to pay off our credit card debt and then—"

"I get it! So just sign the paper, Agnes."

I wave my fork at him. "But it's church! I'd be officially lying in church."

"But you don't believe in God."

I shake my head, pull the empty coffee cake box toward me, and start stabbing the top of it. "You make it sound so easy."

"You asked for help," Mo is saying. "And I'm helping. Logic is your friend—even if you're not a friend to logic."

I keep stabbing the plastic. "Some things are not always logical."

— Chapter 9 —

BY THE TIME MO'S MOM AND HIS SISTER SADIE PULL INTO the driveway, Mo has finished his half of the coffee cake and the rest of my half, too.

I, on the other hand, have managed to completely destroy the lid of the box.

"Good job taking care of the evidence," Mo whispers as he wipes up all the remnants and puts them in the trash. "Even if she goes through the garbage, she'll never recognize it."

There's the jangle of the key in the lock, and then Mo's mom sweeps into the house like she always does: talking a mile a minute with her arms full of groceries and Sadie's school stuff. Sadie trails behind her doing twirls and then bunny hops away into the living room.

"Agnes! How are you? How was your day?" Mo's mom asks. "Are you hungry? I just got new snacks at the grocery store."

"It was good, and I'm full, thanks," I say.

Mo clears his throat. "Don't forget about your only son! My day was fine, and actually, yes, I could use a snack."

Honestly, Mo could win awards with his metabolism. He must get it from his dad, who takes about eight peanut butter and jelly sandwiches with him to work every day.

Mo's mom squeezes him into a hug from behind. "No snacks right before dinner, but I'm glad your day was good."

Mo starts looking through the grocery bags. "What's for dinner?"

"Just pasta and sauce tonight, and you're going to be watching Sadie," she says. "Your dad and I have trivia night and need to leave by 6:00 p.m." She smiles. "Our team is doing great!"

I try to remember the last time my mom went out with friends. Or even talked to someone on the phone. Between work and her night classes, I think it's been years.

Mo starts to say something, but then Sadie flies into the room. "I AM A DINOSAUR FAIRY!" she screams. She leaps into the air and comes down hard. She leaps again and lands with another big thump. "I AM TERRIFYING. I WILL EAT YOU ALL." She spins until she falls over.

"Dinosaur Fairy, can you get your lunch stuff from your backpack and put it in the sink?" Mo's mom asks. She's already gotten two bags of groceries put away.

"DINOSAUR FAIRIES ARE VERY BUSY!" Sadie yells.

"Your lunch stuff, please," Mo's mom says.

Sadie leaps again, but instead of getting her lunch stuff, she hops right over her backpack.

Mo's mom shakes her head and giggles under her breath. "She did this for the entire dance class. Everyone else was practicing first and second position, and she was leaping around and thumping."

"Are you going to stop bringing her to class?" Mo asks.

She shakes her head. "She's six. She's allowed to be silly. Will you unpack the rest of these groceries?"

"I can help, too," I say and start to unload a bag.

"Thank you, Agnes," she says. "You know, Mo was telling me you started confirmation classes. It's wonderful you're doing that."

"Yeah, it's real wonderful, right, Agnes?" Mo jokes.

"I'm serious, Mo," his mom says. "Sometimes I regret not raising you as Jewish. If we had, you'd be learning Hebrew and getting ready for your bar mitzvah right now. You'd be preparing to be an adult."

"I've got six years until I'm an adult, Mom," Mo says.

She nods. "And if you wait to start thinking about your future till then, it'll be too late."

Mo glances at her. "That's a little harsh, don't you think?"

His mom shakes her head. "I know you want to resist this, but your dad is right. A good college is how you get a good job, and a good resume is how you get into a good college, and colleges will be looking for *serious* students who are dedicated and members of teams and—"

"And high school is too late to start a new sport," Mo finishes for her. "I know."

When she goes back out to the car for more grocery bags, Mo sighs. "She's fixated on the path to college stuff."

I pull a box of pasta out of the bag. "It's all right. You don't really care about opopinions, right?"

Mo smirks. "Too bad parents always want us to care about theirs."

I let out a deep breath. "Yeah. And what are we supposed to do then?"

Just then, Mo's mom reappears, with more grocery bags and a flyer. "Mo, I almost forgot. I got more information about that basketball camp. It sounds perfect!"

Mo drops the empty grocery bag over his head. "Then how about *you* go to it."

Mo and I crack up when his mom gets that deer in head-lights look.

Chapter 10

AT HOME, I FLOP DOWN ONTO MY BED. THINGS WOULD be so much easier if I could convince myself to believe in God. But every time I think about how angry He was in those early Bible stories, I feel bad. Because why would that kind of God love me? And where are the girls in the Bible stories who get to feel God's love—without having to die? Or without biting apples that condemn the whole human race for eternity? I thought believing in God was supposed to feel good, not like you're digging yourself even deeper into a hole.

Just then, my phone buzzes in my hand. It's a video of Sadie from Mo. She now plans to try out for our school's annual spring talent show with her own dance routine, and there she is in their kitchen swinging her arms around like she's a robotic windmill in a tornado.

I laugh in spite of myself. That girl—I just love her confidence! So many kids seem more sure of themselves than I'll ever be. Last year at the talent show, Miranda played the piano, and a bunch of her friends did a full dance routine to a Beyoncé song. The whole auditorium exploded when they finished. What would that feel like to be up there on that stage?

I start scrolling through my phone, watching different music videos, imagining what it'd be like to pull off one of those dance routines. I end up clicking on the trailer for a Beyoncé documentary. There isn't any music in the trailer, though. Just a voice that sounds old and wise and kind. An interviewer asks the question: "And what advice would you have to give this generation?"

And the old, wise, kind voice says: "Tell the truth. To yourself first."

I click stop on the video. I feel like time has stopped. Like the voice is speaking right to me.

Because I've never considered that someone could be lying to themselves.

And I've never felt so swept away by a voice before. I do a Google search to find out the voice on the Beyoncé trailer is Maya Angelou. It says the quote is from one of her last interviews before she died in 2014.

Maya Angelou. I swear I've seen her name before. And suddenly, I realize where.

I burst out of my room and into my mom's room and pull open her closet door.

And there she is on a poster pinned to the inside of my mom's closet door. At the bottom of the poster are the words, "Still, like dust, I'll rise."

I feel like I can hear Maya Angelou saying those words in her beautiful voice.

— Chapter 11 —

"MOM," I SAY AS SOON AS I'VE GOTTEN TO THE KITCHEN. "You have a poster of Maya Angelou."

She looks up from the bills she's been paying at the kitchen table. "Why do you look so shocked?"

"I guess because I didn't really know who she was before. She's . . ." How do I describe it? And why do I feel like my heart wants to leap out of my chest? Was it her voice? No, not just her voice . . . it was her voice saying what she said.

"She's an amazing writer." My mom completes the sentence for me. "I must have gotten that poster in college. I was an English major, and I remember reading her autobiography for one of my classes, and it was wonderful. Really inspiring."

"What'd she talk about in her autobiography?" I ask. "I know one of the things she said was that the most important thing was to tell the truth. To yourself first."

"Did she?" my mom says, looking up at the clock. "We should start getting dinner ready. We're having stir-fry tonight."

She heads to the fridge. "Snap peas were too expensive, but

I got green peppers and onions and carrots." She emerges with them all in hand. "Oh, and a can of pineapple. I was thinking we could try that sweet-and-sour sauce again. Can you be in charge of the pineapples and the carrots? I'll do the onions and peppers."

"Sure," I say, retrieving the can of pineapples from the cupboard. I try again. "What do you remember from her autobiography?"

But my mom's looking at her phone and doesn't seem interested in this conversation. I guess just because she used to be excited about Maya Angelou doesn't mean she is anymore.

"Oh dear," she says. "I missed a call from Gracy. I hope everything's okay."

She starts to listen to the voice message and glances at me, confused. "I think she's inviting you over to show you something? Something about an opossum—no idea what that could be—"

"Yes! Can I go?" I'm up and almost out the door when I remember our stir-fry plans. I glance at the can of pineapples on the counter. "I mean . . ."

"Go ahead." My mom smiles. "Grandma Agnes isn't close by, and those kinds of relationships are important. I'll make the stir-fry on my own."

"Are you sure?"

My mom turns on the radio to the news and nods. "I'm sure. She seems like such a sweet old lady."

Chapter 12

WHEN I GET TO GRACY'S DOOR, THERE'S AN OFFICIAL-looking note stuck to it with a message about the trees in her front yard.

"What's that?" I ask, pointing to it when she comes to the door.

"Oh, nothing to worry about," she says, glancing at it. "Some of our neighbors are concerned about whether my new birch trees are allowed by the new neighborhood association rules. I don't know what they have against beautiful trees . . . Anyway, come in! I have something to show you!"

She leads me inside to the dining room. The table is piled with old magazines, books, and travel guides. The other end of the table is cleared except for . . .

"Is that a skull?!"

Gracy grins. "It sure is. And not just any skull. That, my friend, is an opossum skull."

"But where did you . . ."

"I have a few different skulls stored in the basement that I've collected over the years—and I just remembered one was an opossum. I found it way back when I was getting my anthropology PhD." She motions me over. "Come on, it's not going to bite. Take a closer look."

I step forward. "It's so long and pointy."

"Isn't it, though? It looks like the ancient animal it is."

"Sixty million years old, right?" I say.

"Good memory." Gracy's eyes twinkle. "Contemporaries with the saber-toothed cat."

The line between the opossum's forehead and its nose is such a smooth curve. Like the kind of long gentle sledding hill Mo is always searching for. "Can I touch it?"

"Sure can. All the germs were boiled away long ago."

I run my finger along that slope to its mouth. "Those sharp teeth must have helped it last so long, too."

"Well, the teeth help them eat anything. But the most important thing is their ability to take care of their babies."

I look up at her. "Isn't survival more about your ability to defend yourself against enemies?"

Gracy snorts. "A world history textbook might make you think that, but no species survives if it can't raise healthy babies. And opossum mothers can raise nearly forty babies a year."

"Forty? How's that even possible? But I guess there were a lot in that pouch."

Gracy walks to a bookshelf that's threatening to collapse under the weight of all its books. She pulls one out and starts reading aloud. "'Thirteen spots in the pouch for nursing, and up to three litters of babies a year.'" She hands me the book.

"That's a lot of babies." I peer at the picture of the opossum and the close-up of one of its hands. "It looks just like a human hand."

"Yes, they have opposable thumbs, too, which come in handy." Gracy smiles. "Agnes, what do you think was the biggest reason humans developed into a dominant species?"

"Uh . . ." I think of Mo sideways leaping down the sidewalk like his version of a caveman. "Using tools to hunt?"

"The human version of sharp teeth, eh?" Gracy clears the books off two chairs, and we sit down. "Tools and weapons helped, but the real game changer was our big brains. Our ability to work together, make plans, debate options, and divide up tasks made us an unstoppable force."

"Like how cavemen hunted in groups?"

She pauses. "That's what comes to your mind first, isn't it? How about the women? What do you think they were doing?"

"Uh . . ." I don't want to admit I kind of assumed they were waiting back at the cave.

Gracy shakes her head. "It's not your fault you only picture the men. That's the story you've been told because for a long time the only anthropologists were men, and they weren't as interested in talking about women's roles. But let's change that image in your head right now." She leans toward me. "Because you know who found ways to birth those big-brained humans? Women who asked other women for help when they were in labor. You know what formed the cornerstone for human relationships and ultimately for societies? The bond between a woman and her child. Who developed language? Women reassuring their babies with their voices. Who likely invented the first calendar? Women tracking the cycles of the moon." Gracy pauses. "Guess who provided most of the food."

My head is swirling. "That one was men, right?" I venture. "With their hunting?"

Gracy raises her eyebrows. "It was the women who made baskets from grass and gathered plants and berries. It was the women who wove string nets and caught small game and fish. That was far more reliable than going up against a big wild animal."

It's like Gracy has turned on an enormous light bulb inside my head. And the more stuff she tells me, the more my mind is blown.

"How do you know all of this?" I blurt. And why does it feel so huge?

Gracy goes back over to her bookshelf and pulls another book off the shelf. "Thankfully, the field of anthropology has been busy making up for lost time. She hands me a fat book published by the Smithsonian, then starts piling magazines on top, *National Geographic* and *Scientific American* and *American Anthropologist*.

"Always remember," she says, "we can never understand the truth about something if we don't wonder what we're missing. Metal spears will easily turn up at an archeological site, but intricately woven grass baskets won't necessarily survive."

"I've never thought of that, but of course it makes sense," I say.

"You see, Agnes, underestimating women has been a habit for generations." Gracy shakes her head. "People always say that it's hard to change someone's mind, but it's even harder to change someone's habits." She taps the opossum skull. "Just ask our friend here."

I touch the edge of the opossum's jawbone at the base of one of its sharpest teeth. "Maybe opossums will evolve so that they stop playing dead when they're in a road," I say quietly.

Gracy puts a hand on mine. "It just takes enough of them finding a way," she says. "And then they've reshaped the future."

THE OPINION OF AN OPOSSUM

Maybe sometimes we have to play dead, but you know what's kept us opossums going since the time of the dinosaurs? How us mamas can carry our babies around with us. All seasons of the year. Over all sorts of obstacles.

And how great are we at sniffing out food? Yep. We're unstoppable when it comes to finding what's edible, no matter where it might be.

Single mothers for the win.

You think opossums have a story about some female opossum screwing things up because she took a bite of a shiny apple in a garden?

Not a chance.

— Chapter 13 —

"SO, WHAT WAS IT GRACY WANTED TO SHOW YOU?" MY
mom asks over dinner.

"An opossum skull."

She pauses with her fork raised in the air. "Well, that's sure
unexpected. Was it interesting?"

"It actually was," I tell her. "Did you know opossums have
played dead for millions of years just so their predators will
leave them alone?"

"Is that so?" my mom murmurs between bites.

"But now their predators are cars, so they're just getting run
over."

She looks at me. "That's rough."

"They should change, right?" I say. "They should stop playing dead. At least when they're in traffic."

"They probably should."

"They probably will. It's just, change takes time . . ."

"I don't know." My mom takes a bite. "Does an opossum
even know it's possible to change?"

I stop chewing. "I hope so."

My mom doesn't look up from her food, but something has woken up inside me, and I press on. "Gracy's really interesting. She knows a lot about ancient women and all the important things they did—they actually gathered most of the food and figured out how to use stones to grind grains and how to fish with nets and stuff. It's kind of amazing, right?"

"Really? That's nice." My mom says through a yawn. "I'm sorry, Agnes. I had to get up early to study for my accounting class."

And that's the end of our conversation. My mom doesn't have enough time in a day to do all her work or get proper sleep or have friends. So it's not like she has time to think about what women were achieving thousands of years ago. Or to suddenly want to question all sorts of things you've always assumed were true.

But that doesn't mean I have to be the same.

THE OPINION OF AN OPOSSUM

What do you do if your mama, who has carried you and fed you for your whole life, thinks you should both keep playing dead? What if she doesn't think there's another option?

What if she's wrong?

The mama opossum walks and walks, carrying her young. But if those babies keep clinging on forever, if they stay with her every step of the way . . . would they ever have the chance to evolve?

Instead, when they're old enough, they need to drop off, hit the ground, and start making decisions for themselves.

But that moment when you let go of her fur and start falling to the ground? It's terrifying.

—— Chapter 14 ——

"I'M NOT GOING TO SIGN THE FORM," I TELL MO AT LUNCH the next day. "It feels too much like lying."

"Good for you," he says.

"Right. Good for me. It's just a piece of paper anyhow."

I glance at Miranda's table and feel a pang. But maybe Miranda and Pastor Paul won't even care about what I do. Maybe my mom is just worried about how all this church stuff will affect her shot at that promotion for nothing. Maybe it's the unknown that's the worst of it. Just like that moment when an opossum lets go of her mother.

But what happens if she lets go just as her mom's running across a highway? That terrifying freefall would be nothing compared to what was coming.

A balled-up straw wrapper lands on my tray. I glance up. The boys one table over aren't looking at us, but their shoulders are shaking with laughter. Mo has charted how often we're the recipient of balled-up straw wrappers. One out of every ten school days on average. Down from one out of five last year. But then, Mo towers over most of those boys now.

Mo, of course, isn't bothered. He just takes out his notebook so he can update his chart.

"When did you decide you weren't going to care about opopinions?" I ask him.

He shrugs. "I think I was born this way."

Was I born *this* way? Was I worrying about what other people thought from inside the womb? Or maybe it just got kneaded into me at every turn.

"I'm sick of caring about what other people think. Half of them are fake anyway," I say. "People that smile at you when they don't mean it." I glare at the backs of the boys. "People who pretend to be innocent when they're not."

Mo takes out his bag of thinly sliced apples. "So you prefer people that glare at you and brag about all the bad things they've done."

I flick the straw wrapper at Mo and picture Rick Adams. "And I'm sick of people who have more power than they should."

Mo squishes the straw wrapper between his fingers. "I bet *those* people don't care too much about opopinions."

"You're probably right, Mo. And you know what else you were right about? St. Agnes always having a sheep with her on all my grandmother's cards."

Mo nods. He peels the top off his yogurt.

"Did you know she died in a horrible way?" I say.

"Who?"

"St. Agnes. I found out she lived about seventeen hundred years ago."

"You're full of all sorts of interesting tidbits today." He begins to devour his yogurt.

Even though I don't want to think about her, for some reason it's annoying me that Mo doesn't even seem to care. "You know that when she was only twelve or thirteen she was dragged through the streets and beheaded?"

Mo grimaces without looking up from his yogurt. "Harsh. What'd she do?"

"What do you mean?" I ask. "And it's way worse that just harsh!"

"I mean, what'd she do to get them to drag her through the street?"

"I read it was because she was a devout Christian and that she refused to marry some guy."

"She probably did something else, too," Mo says.

I open my mouth. Then I close it. Part of me wants to whack Mo's yogurt container out of his hand, but I try to stay calm.

"You know," Mo says, leaning back in his chair, "I don't understand how anyone could get dragged someplace. Your feet are right there on the ground. Why don't you just use them to go in the direction that you want to?"

I look at him. Does he really need me to explain this to him?

"Because someone stronger than you is dragging you by the arms in the opposite direction."

"But if you really wanted to go in the opposite direction,

don't you think you could make that happen? Like if you really, really wanted to."

I feel my voice rising. "But sometimes you don't have any control. No matter how much you want it."

The boys from the table over start laughing. Evidently, I spoke loudly. One of them looks at me and covers his mouth in pretend horror. They think they can make me feel weird. Well, I already feel weird—it doesn't matter what they do.

I get up the nerve and give them my best glare. I glare until they finally turn around. Even though I still want to whack Mo's yogurt container out of his hand, I feel victorious.

I exhale. Maybe some people have more power than I do, but that doesn't mean I don't have any.

— Chapter 15 —

THERE'S STILL SOME TIME BEFORE CLASS STARTS, SO I tell Mo there's something I have to do, and I head to the library. It's quiet when I get there, and when I ask Ms. Sawyer if they have any books about Maya Angelou, she smiles.

"One of my heroes. We've got a couple great books about her. Follow me."

A few minutes later, I'm sitting at one of the tables with two volumes of poetry and a picture book biography about her called *Rise*, which Ms. Sawyer suggested I take, saying, "Picture books are for everyone."

I flip open the picture book first. Maya Angelou looks so strong on my mom's poster, but here she's just an everyday kid. So I start reading it, looking to see how she became so strong and confident.

But it's not what I expect because it seems like it was hardships that made her so strong. Not only did she have to deal with a racist society, but when she was a girl, a man attacked her, and after she told the truth about what happened, that man was found dead. To her it felt like her voice had killed him, and she stopped talking. To everyone but her brother.

But then how did she become so convinced that telling the truth was the right thing to do? How did she get to a place where she could write, *Still, like dust, I'll rise*?

The bell rings, and Ms. Sawyer calls over to me. "Agnes, would you like to check those books out?"

I scramble up from my seat. "Yes, I would."

▲●■

At home that afternoon, I don't even grab a snack. I sit down at the kitchen table, take out the picture book, and flip right to the page where Maya was sitting with her knees pulled up against her, not talking. I turn the page to see what happens next, and suddenly it feels obvious. The way she survives is with stories. Her stories and ideas may not have anything to do with shopping carts or opossums, but there's something familiar about the words filling her head. Because they're reminders that the world is bigger than the one she's living in. That her body might be trapped, but her head and heart don't have to be.

Then one day, she starts to read aloud to herself, and that's when everything starts to change. Because she recognizes that her voice, released out into the open, has power.

Her confidence spills over and she becomes a writer and a poet and a dancer and a singer. And she works to make the world less unfair. At the end of the book, she's reading her work at a presidential inauguration in front of the whole country.

When I get to the last page, I go back to the beginning and read it again.

The next book turns out to be an illustrated version of a poem called "Life Doesn't Frighten Me." It doesn't? But she lists so many scary things in the poem and says she refuses to scream, refuses to cry. Instead, she smiles and makes *them* turn and run. I'd like to be able to do that!

I save the collection of poetry for later and look out the window at the rows of identical houses. My life is different from Maya Angelou's in so many ways. But it feels like there's so much I can learn from her. I like how she was able to see beyond the boundaries other people built. And one brave act at a time, she rose right over those boundaries.

▲●■

When my mom comes home, she disappears into her bedroom to change out of her skirt and stockings as usual.

I think about how she was once inspired by Maya Angelou and even kept her poster. I want to ask her why she keeps it hidden in her closet, but I'm pretty sure I know the answer— Mom's all about not messing up our beige walls.

When she returns in her pajama pants, I ask a different question even though I probably know the answer to that one, too. "Why do you wear a skirt and stockings every day even though you hate them?"

"Sometimes what you want isn't as important as what you need," she tells me.

I nod. We need her job. We need her salary. We need a place

to live and food to eat. And we really need her to get that promotion so we can finally pay off our credit card bill with my braces on it.

But what if you feel like you need more than that?

When my mom starts pulling stuff out of the fridge for dinner, I go into her room and look up at the poster of Maya Angelou. Her eyes . . . they are kind, but they are also so certain. This is a person who is brave enough to look the truth in the face, no matter how hard it is. Brave enough to leap even if she's not sure where she'll land. Brave enough to stride forward without a second glance at the judgments of others.

Just knowing there are people like that gives me a new kind of courage.

— Chapter 16 —

ON SATURDAY AFTERNOON, I VOLUNTEER TO MOW
Gracy's lawn. Which I'd want to do anyway so that I can see
her but will also count as community service for confirmation
class.

When I get there, there's another warning slip stuck to
Gracy's door. Gracy crumples it up as soon as she opens the
door.

"They really don't like your trees, do they?" I say.

"No, and now they're also complaining about my compost
bin even though it's in the backyard out of sight unless you
stand at just the right angle."

"Why do they care about that?" I ask.

She smirks as she leads me to the garage, where her lawn
mower is kept. "They probably think wolves are going to come
eat my onion peels." She winks at me. "And of course, if it happened to attract one of our tick-eating marsupial friends, they
should be thanking me."

After I finish mowing, Gracy gives me water with some herby things from her garden. I drink the water slow, trying to dodge the leafy bits as I go.

"Do you like confirmation class?" she asks.

"It's okay." Then I correct myself: "I mean, yes." Who knows how religious Gracy is?

"So it's just okay, but you're determined to like it anyway?"

I feel my face get hot and decide to tell her the truth. "It's annoying that almost all the stories in the Bible are about men." I poke at the leafy bits in my water. "Last time you said we have a habit of underestimating women from the past. Why does that happen?"

"History is a story," she says. "A story based on facts if the writer's done their research and weighed all the evidence, but a story nonetheless. So you always need to be thinking about who's telling the story."

I nod even though I'm not sure what she's talking about. I always thought history was history. I don't think our social studies textbook even lists an author.

Gracy looks at me. "For the last two thousand years, who's been telling the story?"

"What do you mean?"

"Who were the leaders? Who were the academics? Who were the translators? Who were the monks who copied the books?"

"I . . ." I trail off. I don't have a clue.

Gracy stands up. "They were men."

She walks over to a desk piled with papers and starts digging through the mess. "Here!" she exclaims. "Look at this. I brought this photo to my archeology club." She sets it in front of me. "That," she says, "is the Ziggurat of Ur, one of the oldest pyramids in Mesopotamia. I took that picture when I was visiting Iraq back in the 80s. Do you know why it was so important to me to go there?"

I study the photo. Mostly, it looks like a pile of bricks. "Because it was old?"

"Because . . ." She pauses for effect. "This was where the oldest known recorded poem in the history of the world was written down. From the year 2300 BCE. One of our first looks at the passions and beliefs of the humans who had been living and thinking and feeling for tens of thousands of years but never leaving a trace of what those thoughts were."

"What was the poem about?" I ask. "Do we know who wrote it?"

She fixes her eyes on me. "It was about God."

I exhale. Of course it was. Of course ancient humans had figured out a way to believe when I don't even know how to start.

"And it was written by high priest En'Hedu'anna."

"So, what does it say about Him?"

Gracy presses her lips together to hold back a smile. "No, Agnes. Not about Him. This God was a Her."

I feel my mouth drop open.

She raises her eyebrows. "And that high priest was a woman."

She says it so matter-of-factly. And then she starts listing all sorts of female Gods from all sorts of religions, and I feel like I'm going to burst right out of myself, leaving little chunks of me all over her kitchen.

I lift my glass of water, and I down it in one swig. Leafy bits and all.

THE OPINION OF AN OPOSSUM

Some people say we look like big rats. And no one decorates their baby's rooms with our faces. No one starts campaigns about protecting us and our habitat.

What does that say? It says we're not important.

But that's not the whole story! We might not matter to many people, but maybe what those folks think about us *isn't* important.

Because we were here before them, and we just might be here after them, too.

No matter what they say.

— Chapter 17 —

AT CHURCH THE NEXT MORNING, I REACH INTO MY POCKET to touch the list of female gods Gracy helped me make yesterday, some from the past and some current ones, too. Pastor Paul is up at the pulpit leading us in prayer, but all I can think about is what it'd be like if all those He pronouns were She.

"He who is all-powerful and all-knowing, let us pray to Him so that He may hear our prayers."

She *who is all-powerful and all-knowing, let us pray to* Her *so that* She *may hear our prayers.*

When we stand and sing "Praise My Soul, the King of Heaven," I silently mouth Her for every Him. Queen for every King . . .

Her *feet thy tribute bring . . .*

Praise Her *for* Her *grace . . .*

Yes, my words may be silent.

But right now,

in this moment,

they feel world changing.

As soon as I get home from church, I text Mo.

> You know what's amazing?
> When u change all the male pronouns 2 female in church!
> Imagine God as a She!
> Shakes your worldview up, doesn't it?

But he doesn't write back. For the entire day!

I keep checking my phone. Is he angry? Does he think it's anti-man?

Am I anti-man?

I don't think so. I just want to be pro-myself.

Still, I think about the way I just left Mo at lunch on Friday to go to the library. And how I was so busy reading about Maya Angelou that I didn't text him as much on Saturday as I usually do. And how now that I think about it, his texts made it seem like he was kind of sad.

> I'm sorry about the way I left at lunch on Friday, I text. Your shopping cart story is really great so far. Super funny.

My phone sits there. No buzzing. Screen black.

> I think you'd really like Maya Angelou
> She doesn't beat around the bush. Just says it like it is.

He still doesn't respond. *Don't freak out,* I tell myself. But imagining life without Mo means instantly freaking out.

And then, finally, I remember. Mo's family was going to his

cousin's college graduation today, and his mom doesn't let him take his phone for family events. Phew!

▲ ● ■

That night, he does text me back, but he doesn't say anything about what I've written. Or about the graduation. He just quotes more of his shopping cart story to me . . .

> Steve was all alone in the park and the rain was falling hard. He pictured the spot in front of the grocery store where all the other carts waited, protected from the rain. Maybe he did belong at the grocery store. Maybe he did want The Hands to bring him back inside.

I'm about to text him back to stop and to actually respond to what I wrote, but then more of his story shows up . . .

> It was helpful The Hands were plural, so no one had to figure out pronouns: just a simple all-powerful They.

I sigh and turn off my phone. Is Mo making progress? Does he get what I'm trying to say? And if he does, why does everything still have to be about shopping carts?

— Chapter 18 —

ON MONDAY MORNING, I FIND MO BEFORE SCHOOL starts. Ever since the principal told us big kids to stay off the playground before school, Mo's been hanging out near the portable classroom, where he likes to pick at the soft, sticky tar that's used to patch the cracks in the blacktop and pop the bubbles. He says he finds it oddly comforting. Plus, he thinks he can estimate the temperature based on how soft it is.

I drop my backpack next to him.

"Hey!" he says when he sees me. "You didn't write back! Didn't you like the shopping cart excerpts I sent you?"

I shake my head. "Well, you didn't answer my texts either."

"Which texts?"

"God, men, women, all that stuff? Mo! Pay attention. This is important to me!" I say it louder than I mean to. A group of third graders look up from their game of four square.

"I know it is," he says. "It's like me and basketball."

"What? No. How?"

"It's like you're being erased. Didn't you read all of my story?"

I shake my head. "I don't know. I might have turned off my phone."

Mo pulls a paper from his backpack and starts to read.

"It was helpful The Hands were plural so no one had to figure out pronouns: just a simple all-powerful They. But suddenly Steve thought a bigger thought than he'd ever thought before.

The Hands might push Steve around, but that didn't mean there wasn't something out there bigger than The Hands. And if there was, he wanted to imagine it as a giant, glowing shopping cart. Because why not? Why wouldn't the God of Shopping Carts look like a shopping cart?"

I feel my mouth open slightly. "You do get it," I whisper.

"Well, it did take me a bit, but then I got there. First, I was thinking God could be the wind or even the bread. Hey, maybe I can do metaphors after all." He pushes at the tar with his finger. "I tell you, Agnes, this shopping cart story is a keeper. Even if it has some random tangents."

I watch the tar give way gently. "I always like the tangents, Mo. That's the beauty of those stories."

"Yeah, it can be good to end up in a different place than you were expecting."

The warning bell rings, and Mo picks up his backpack. "Can

you come to the auditions after school today?" he asks. "I've got to take Sadie."

"Sure," I tell him. "I bet it'll be packed, but no way I'd miss her dance routine." Kids get pretty excited about the talent show, and there are always so many trying out that they need to hold two days of auditions. I open the weather app on my phone. "So, what's your guess?"

"Sixty-four degrees."

"Close! Sixty-five."

"Ah, I wonder if there's ever been anyone with such mad skills at Sticky Tar Poking!"

I stand up slowly. "Maybe they'll put up a monument to you in the park."

"Yes!" Mo exclaims. "And the inscription will read: *Remember Mo, Who Discovered New Ways to Understand Things.*"

"I'll visit it," I say.

"No, you'll be dead by then, but you'll have your own monument, too. It'll be as big as mine, and they can face each other. Like we do when we're playing double solitaire. What's yours going to say?"

"I have no idea."

"Well, you've got to get on that then," Mo says.

— Chapter 19 —

THAT AFTERNOON, MO AND I FOLLOW SADIE INTO THE auditorium and watch as she joins the crowd of kids near the stage waiting to audition.

I nudge Mo. "You sure you don't want to try out?"

"And do what?" he says as we find some seats. "Go on stage, hold up a notebook of writing, and then bow enthusiastically as everyone claps?"

I raise my eyebrows. "Read, silly!"

"Right." Mo snorts. "I've got a better idea. How about we start writing together again so we can submit something for the newspaper contest? Doesn't my shopping cart story make you want to get back to it?"

I sigh. "Mo, we've been over this before. I'm not ready. Why don't you submit what you've been working on—without me?"

Mo presses his lips together. "But it's not the same."

I sigh. "I know. But it wasn't *always* going to be the same anyway. One of us was going to get tired sooner or later."

Right then, the teacher in charge of the auditions quiets

everyone and gets things started. None of the group acts seem too nervous, but whenever someone performs all by themselves, it's a different story. A bunch of kids forget their lines or speak so softly it makes my stomach curl to watch them.

When it's Sadie's turn, I'm worried for her, but as soon as the music starts, she's up there spinning and dancing her heart out. Where does she get that confidence?

"Have you seen this dance before?" I whisper to Mo.

Mo shakes his head. "She likes to keep it fresh. With Sadie you never know what you're going to get."

"Isn't the point of an audition, so they know what they're going to get?" I ask.

"Good luck if that's what they think!"

We give Sadie high fives when she's done, and then she insists on staying to watch the rest of the auditions, and my mom agrees to pick us up on her way home from work.

The last audition slot of the day is Miranda, and by this point it's gotten noisy with parents arriving for pickup.

This year, instead of playing piano, Miranda sings a song I remember from Sunday school, except that this version has a better beat that she kind of half dances to while she sings. She hits all the notes, but her voice trembles. At least Tya and her other friends are there cheering her on, and when she gets off the stage, they all pile onto her in a hug.

"You did it," I hear Tya say. "See? You didn't have to be nervous. You're totally going to be a star!"

Miranda swallows and nods. "Really? I'm still shaking."

"Lots of kids get nervous, but you powered through," says Tya.

Then Miranda gets enveloped by another group hug.

I guess what Tya said is right—it doesn't matter how nervous anyone is, as long as they still get up on that stage and do their thing.

— Chapter 20 —

AFTERWARD, SADIE, MO, AND I WAIT FOR MY MOM TO arrive in our spot behind the hedges. We discovered this spot when both of our moms insisted on signing us up for first-grade soccer. Even though we tolerated soccer because of the orange wedges at the game, the practices had nothing going for them. We'd ask to go inside to use the bathroom in the middle of practice, and then we'd hang out here, hidden by the hedges, for as long as we could.

"How were you so confident for that audition?" I ask Sadie.

She looks at me like I just asked her how she got her arms. "Because it's just dancing, you know."

It's like she's straight out of that Maya Angelou poem. Life doesn't frighten Sadie at all.

She starts telling us about how cool ants are when Miranda walks by with her dad, who sounds like he's giving her a lecture.

"That isn't who we are," Rick Adams is saying. "That is not who *you* are."

Through the hedge, I see Miranda wipe her eyes. Wow, she's

crying. "I don't understand," she says. "I thought you were okay with me trying out."

"To sing that song we agreed on," Rick Adams says. "Not to inappropriately dance along to it."

"But I thought I did okay."

Her dad pauses. "Do you want people like Pastor Paul to see you gyrating like that?"

Gyrating? Other than Miranda keeping time to the music with her hips, there was not much shaking going on.

When Miranda tries to defend herself, her father cuts her off. "Let's not ever have it happen again," he tells her. "Now cheer up, it's almost time for dinner and Aunt Deborah made baked ziti."

Miranda slowly follows behind her father, and suddenly all I can think about is how lonely she looks. She doesn't look like she feels God's love. What if deep down, she's as confused as I am about it all?

Why can't God be someone who encourages us to be who we are? Who listens to our most secret dreams and then gives us a fist bump and tells us to go for it? Who has our back, not because it's required, but because God knows what doubt feels like and isn't going to let us doubt ourselves? Why can't we picture God that way? Why can't we picture God as someone who's wise and loves fiercely and stands up for the underdog?

Because that is a God I could believe in.

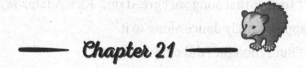

— *Chapter 21* —

AFTER DINNER, MY PHONE BUZZES IN MY POCKET. IT'S Mo texting.

I found something 4 u.

What's he talking about?

The Internet is a magical place.
It'll be here in 3–5 business days.
You're welcome.

I stare at my phone and then type in, It better not have anything to do with sheep. But I don't send it. I'm going to let Mo have his moment to be mysterious.

▲ ● ■

My mom is still at the kitchen table, so I head into her room and open her closet. Somehow, seeing Maya Angelou calms me. I keep thinking about how she was able to stay strong no matter what life threw at her.

I study every inch of her face. Her high forehead. The curve of her nose. Her mouth so determined.

Those words she wrote—and then spoke aloud:

> *You may trod me in the very dirt.*
> *But still, like dust, I'll rise.*

My mind flashes to St. Agnes, and I picture her being dragged through the streets. How did she get through that? How could anyone?

I take my phone out and look up more information on St. Agnes. There's all the stuff I read on the cards about how she always has a lamb and how she's the patron saint of girls and chastity. But there's a ton more about her death. She wasn't just dragged through the streets and then beheaded. She was dragged through the streets NAKED. And then it was said that her hair magically grew long and covered her body while she was being dragged. So they decided she must be a witch and tried to burn her at the stake, but the fire wouldn't ignite. THEN they chopped her head off with a sword.

Seriously? Either the writers had a vivid imagination or really wild things were going on back then.

I take a deep breath and keep reading. I find that there are a bunch of different versions of her story, but the one thing that stays constant is her "crime"—turns out St. Agnes was so devoted to God that she wasn't interested in marrying anyone, no matter what was said or done to her. Maybe her body was dragged, but her mind and her heart were unshakeable.

She may have looked all alone, but I bet she didn't feel that way because she believed God was with her.

Is faith like that really possible? Faith that comes from within yourself rather than from what people tell you to believe? I pick up the card with her picture and look at it with new eyes.

I'm sorry I ever underestimated you, St. Agnes.

— Chapter 22 —

WE GET TO CHURCH LATE FOR MY NEXT CONFIRMATION class. It's definitely my fault. Though I did get in the car without my mom having to physically drag me. But only because I get that when someone bigger drags someone in one direction, it's pretty darn hard to stop it.

There's one parking spot near the entrance, and my mom takes it. "Go, go, go, don't be any later—"

But then she stops because the car next to us, the one I almost scratched when I threw my door open, is Rick Adams's Range Rover convertible. And there is Rick Adams waiting for me to get out of his way so he can climb in.

"Agnes! How are you?" he says. "It's so good to see you're part of Miranda's confirmation class."

He ducks down to look through the passenger-side window. "Hello, Eliza," he says as my mom scrambles to put down the window. The back window goes down before she pushes the right button.

"That was a good meeting this afternoon," he says.

"You're absolutely right." My mom tries to sit up straighter. "We can't have mistakes if we want to keep our customers happy."

He nods. "As soon as I found out what you tellers were doing, I knew we needed to nip it in the bud."

"I'm sorry. I thought that it was protocol to ask customers to come inside for larger transactions. I thought the drive-through line was just for—"

"This is why we went over it at the meeting. Those rules are only for some. If Herb wants to deposit the quarterly country club dues, and he does it every four months, he should be able to do that from the comfort of his car, don't you think?"

"Of course," my mom says, nodding quickly.

So, wait. My mom and the other tellers got in trouble for *following* the protocol this time?

Rick Adams looks at me and smiles. "Isn't it getting late? You better run. You don't want Pastor Paul to doubt your commitment to the church, do you?"

I know I'm not supposed to answer that with all the words spinning inside me. Plus, he's not finished.

"You know how I see it," he calls after me, "it's just like at the bank. When you're late, you're disrespecting the people who got there on time. And in this case, that includes God."

"I'm sorry," I hear my mom say again. His car door slams shut, and his engine starts. I'm almost inside, but I turn to see him reverse out of the parking spot without a word. I sneak a quick peek at my mom. Is she okay?

The glare on the windshield means that I can't see her face. *I'm sorry,* I mouth.

The exact words she just said to him.

I apologize again when I come in late to confirmation class, but Pastor Paul just smiles at me. "It's good to see you, Agnes," he says as he hands me a Bible.

I spy the pledge forms on a side table waiting for us, but thankfully right now we're just talking about the lessons we should be taking from Matthew, Mark, Luke, and John. I flip to the Bible verse being discussed and try to catch my breath.

It's when Pastor Paul says, "In Luke's version of the story of Jesus's birth . . ." that something clicks.

Matthew, Mark, Luke, and John are not just names. These are people telling stories of what happened—and they all have different versions of the story. I think of Gracy telling me to pay attention to who's telling the stories.

I skim the story. There's a part about Jesus teaching in a synagogue on the Sabbath. A woman whose body had been bent by a spirit asks to be healed, and even though the people around him were against it, Jesus healed her, and she stood tall for the first time.

I press my lips together and keep reading. Even with a man telling the story, even with so many men dominating the Bible, you can still tell that Jesus respected women. He's way different from the God in the Old Testament.

I close my eyes. Suddenly I want to believe in God more than ever. I want to believe that even though people have been assuming things about Eve and girls and women for thousands of years, that doesn't mean it has to be that way. I want to believe that there exists a force for good that's bigger than all of this.

I want to believe it's possible for my mom and me to stop apologizing so much, too.

▲●■

And at the end of class, when Pastor Paul hands out Miranda's pledge form, I take it. There's just one line of text on the page:

I, _____, solemnly make this pledge that I believe in God the Father and am here to serve Him.

Followed by a line for our signature.

I write my name in the blank, and before I can stop myself, I make a tiny little asterisk after "God the Father" and then two more after "Him." Then, I take out my notebook from my bag, flip to a page in the back, and quickly write:

* or God the Mother, or just God.
** or Her

I look up to see Pastor Paul collecting the forms. He steps closer to me, and I snap my notebook shut.

"I love that this is so important to you," he says, "that you're writing about it in your journal!"

He's looking at my form and its asterisks. I hold my breath.

"Are you going to sign it?" he asks, pushing it closer to me.

He doesn't look angry.

"Yes," I say. Because now I can.

I sign my name in big bold letters.

Pastor Paul smiles. "I like how you decorated it with stars. It's like how each of us is one of God's stars, twinkling away in the universe."

I take one last look at my asterisks twinkling away and hand him the form. "Exactly like that," I say.

I am good. I am golden, even.

And no one else needs to know.

— Chapter 23 —

I'M AT MO'S HOUSE ON SATURDAY TUCKING INTO A BOWL of cereal when Mo bounds up to me after getting the mail. "It came fast!" he shouts.

"What came?"

He waves a big padded envelope in my face. "Your present!"

My what? But then I remember . . . *just the thing* . . . *3–5 business days* . . . "What'd you get me?"

Mo looks like he's going to burst. "Open it."

I rip open the package and pull out a dark blue tank top.

"It's even your favorite color!" Mo says.

"Thank you?" Why is Mo so excited about this? "Umm, why a tank top?"

"Well, it's going to be summer soon," Mo says, plopping down onto the kitchen stool next to me. "I figured it'd help keep you cool. Especially because you've said church always gets hot."

Church?

"But you haven't seen the best part yet! Open it up so you can see the whole thing."

I unfold the tank top and read the words on it.

GOD IS A WOMAN.

"Mo," I breathe.

"Isn't it perfect?" he says as he pours himself another bowl of cereal. "It's exactly what you were talking about, and then boom! The internet delivers!"

"I don't . . ."

"I can't believe it either," Mo says. "It's almost enough to make me religious."

I look at him. He's so excited about it, giddy even. But my brain has gone straight to one thought and one thought only: *I can never wear this.*

"I can't . . ." I say.

"You can't what?"

"I mean, I love it," I say. Because I do. "Thank you."

"Well, of course you do!" Mo holds up the tank top. "What's not to love?"

I press my lips together. "I can think of a few people who might not love it."

"Well, I didn't get it for them, right?" he says.

"Right. And maybe I can just wear it under a sweatshirt so it'll be my special secret." I picture the asterisks I drew on the pledge form. My personal religion could be based on little stars and hidden tank tops.

"Why? It's too fabulous of a shirt to hide," Mo says as he

devours his cereal. "And isn't the whole reason you love Maya Angelou because she was willing to tell the truth even when it's hard?"

I concentrate on getting the last bits of cereal onto my spoon. "The quote was tell the truth. To yourself. I'm doing that."

"Didn't you say she said, 'Tell the truth. To yourself *first*?' She didn't stop there, did she?"

"But if Miranda's dad sees it, he'll freak out."

"Like I said, who cares?"

I glare at him. "You know my mom finally has a chance at that promotion. We have to care."

"Okay," Mo says. "Okay," he says again more quietly. "I get it."

We eat our cereal in silence.

Finally, Mo stops eating. "What if you just wear it to school and not to church?"

"The girls from my confirmation class are all at school. What if Miranda sees it and tells her dad?"

"But what if she doesn't and it's the most glorious feeling because, finally, you're getting to be who you are and say what you think!"

I look up from my bowl. "Do you really always say what you think?"

He starts bopping back and forth. "I sure do."

I watch him. He's always talking about how he never cares about opopinions, but suddenly I realize . . .

"When?" I ask.

Mo doesn't stop bopping. "What are you talking about?"

"When do you say what you think?"

"All the time."

I take a deep breath. "At school, when do you say what you think . . . to someone who isn't me?"

Mo stops bopping.

"You don't, do you? When have you ever done your caveman sideways leap through the hallway?"

"School isn't exactly conducive to people being themselves," he says.

"Right! And I bet not a single student other than me and Sadie knows about the shopping cart stories."

"No one ever asked me about them."

"I'll tell you what," I say. "We'll find a way for you to truly be yourself in front of other people, and then I'll consider wearing this tank top to school."

Mo's eyes open. "Not just 'consider' it, Agnes. You've got to do it."

"Fine."

"At the same time as me."

"Sure. But only if your way of being you is just as big as wearing this tank top."

"Okay," Mo says. "Now, whether you like it or not, you've got a deal."

— Chapter 24 —

I CATCH UP WITH MO THE FIRST THING MONDAY MORNING. "I know what you should do!" I tell him.

Mo looks up from the tar on the playground blacktop. "Good morning to you, too."

"Mo! You should read your new shopping cart story in the talent show."

Mo's face switches to horror, but I press on. "It's funny! Steve's a great character."

He goes back to poking the tar. "I don't think so."

"What?" I say. "Why?"

"I don't know." He shakes his head. "It isn't meant to be read by other people."

"Wait. You're the one who wants to enter a shopping cart story in the contest. You know that requires people to read it, right?"

Mo presses his lips together and keeps poking.

"Maybe you just need to revise it."

He looks up at me. "What if it's an earlier shopping cart story?"

I drop my backpack on the ground. "But we wrote those other ones together. I have my thing. Your thing needs to be all you."

"But that's the problem . . ." he trails off.

"It's going to be great," I say. "And you've got until tomorrow afternoon when they do the second round of auditions. Just revise it tonight or do whatever you need to do to get it ready."

Mo doesn't look up, and I sit down on the ground next to him. "You know what you could do to get yourself ready? You could practice reading it aloud. Maya Angelou did that, and hearing the words inspired her."

"Maybe," Mo says. "You'd really wear the tank top if I agree to do the audition?"

"I will," I say. "I promise."

Mo swallows. "Okay. I'll do it. Tomorrow it is."

We shake on it. Even though Mo looks as terrified as I feel.

▲ ● ■

That night in my room, the sight of the blue edge of the tank top is enough to make me feel sick. Why did I agree to this? Did I have to be so focused on Mo that I forgot all the ways this could be wrong for me?

Or maybe it *isn't* the wrong thing to do. Maybe I'm just scared, too.

87

I take out my math homework to try to distract myself. But I can't even get started. Instead, I start flipping through my opossum notebook.

My opossum isn't afraid to tell it like it is. Even if it isn't what others want to hear. Because sometimes what's needed is the truth.

Why did I give my opossum that voice? Did I hope deep down her courage would be contagious?

I flip back through the opossum entries, take the advice I gave Mo, and start reading my stories aloud.

Maybe it's with a quiet voice, but it is a voice.

And that is a good place to start.

Chapter 25

ON TUESDAY MORNING, I CHECK THE WEATHER. SUPER hot. The kind of unseasonably hot late April day that makes you wonder how you'll survive August unless you're allowed to morph into a Popsicle. The perfect day to wear a tank top.

I put it on and stand in front of the mirror. I can do this. I just have to keep channeling my inner angry opossum.

And it looks good. The white block letters are so straightforward. Like they naturally line up and spell out these words in this order all the time.

GOD IS A WOMAN

Should I cover it up? At least at first?

But this is who I am, plus it's going to be so hot. And the timing is perfect now. My mom already gave me a kiss goodbye and is in the shower. She knows I'll be gone by the time she gets out.

Before I can think any more about it, I grab my backpack and walk out the door into a beautiful spring day with the big bold words on my tank top exposed for everyone to see.

No one says anything at the bus stop. No one pays attention to me on the bus. Mo must be running late because he's not outside, so I head straight to homeroom, and no one treats me any different there either.

Was it always going to be this easy?

People pass me in the hallway as I head to my first class. Most of them don't even look at me. One or two seem to be reading the words on my tank top—but then they keep walking. No balled-up straw wrappers ping off me. Then I notice a few girls giving me smiles. It's like getting silent fist bumps of support that whisper *Actually, you're okay. The real you, even.*

It's all I can do to keep from sideways leaping down the hallway because Mo is right. This feels AMAZING.

I can't wait to tell Mo. Maybe I can track him down between classes because we usually pass each other in the hall midmorning. But when I wait for him near the water fountain, he doesn't show up. Maybe he's signing up to do the audition after school today with Ms. H? That would make sense, and that's on the other side of the school.

I'm almost late to tech ed when a boy who's in a bunch of Mo's classes comes around the corner. I get up my nerve. "Hey," I call to him. "Have you seen Mo?"

The boy glances at me as he pulls open the gym door. "I don't think he's here today."

I freeze in place. Like a blueberry Popsicle.

Mo chickened out. And he didn't even tell me.

It feels like the floor has dropped out from under me, but I try to stay calm and head for class.

Except when I turn around, there's Miranda, staring directly at my shirt.

Before she turns away, the look on her face makes one thing clear: She does not think this is amazing.

▲ ● ■

During our PowerPoint work in tech ed, I pretend I have to go to the bathroom so I can sneak my phone out of my locker and check it. Sure enough, there's a text from Mo, sent right after homeroom began, when he knew I couldn't get it.

I'm sooooo sorry.

And I am soooooo mad.

Way 2 wait 2 tell me until it was 2 late, I text. I honored our deal and wore the tank top.

I wish I could take it off right now. Why isn't there an undo option in real life?

When I come back to class, Ms. Fuller motions me over before I can take my seat.

"While you were in the bathroom, the main office called for you," she says. "You better get going."

Chapter 26

THE SECRETARY TELLS ME TO SIT IN A CHAIR AND WAIT until Principal Sullivan is ready to see me. I keep my arms wrapped across my chest just in case that has any hope of helping, but who am I kidding? The school probably has a rule about T-shirts with blasphemous sayings in the handbook, and of course Miranda would report me right away. I can't believe I thought it was going to be okay.

By the time Principal Sullivan calls me into her office, my arms are frozen to my chest. I follow her inside like the slow-moving and terrified blueberry Popsicle that I am.

Principal Sullivan sits back at her desk and takes a form out of a drawer. She doesn't look at me. "Do you have another shirt with you?" she asks.

I stare down at my feet. "No."

"No gym clothes?"

I shake my head. "I don't have gym today."

"I expect you to be aware of the rules around dress code violations, but since you clearly need a reminder . . ." She takes out the student handbook and flips it open and slides it over to me. "No tank tops."

Wait, really?

"This is a learning environment. It's not a place to flaunt your body, and it's not a place for the distraction of unnecessary skin. And we certainly can't have bra straps showing all over the place." Principal Sullivan is writing up that form while she talks. Has she looked at me or the words on my tank top at all? Does this really have nothing to do with that and everything to do with my shoulders?

I eye my shoulders. I definitely don't have any bra strap showing. Am I flaunting my shoulders? Is it a distraction? Who gets distracted by a shoulder?

Principal Sullivan picks up her phone. "I've already checked with the nurse and she doesn't have any extra shirts right now, so I'm calling your mom so she can bring you a shirt."

"Please don't!" I blurt out. "My mom's at work. Can't I just go home and get something to wear myself?"

But Principal Sullivan keeps dialing the number. "We do not release children during the school day except to the custody of their parents. This is our procedure for dress code violations if no alternative clothing options exist." She finishes dialing, and I can hear the phone on the other end start ringing. A woman picks up—definitely not my mom because tellers don't have their own phones.

"Yes, this is Principal Sullivan at Whitefield School. I'd like to speak to Eliza Bedeman. It's about her daughter. Yes, I'll wait."

One drip at a time, my Popsicle self is melting away. Every

minute it takes for my mom to come to the phone, I shrink further into the chair as the drip, drip, drips pool at my feet.

"Yes, Eliza, I'm sorry to bother you at work, but your daughter Agnes has violated our dress code, and you need to bring in a new shirt for her to wear."

Principal Sullivan listens as my mom says something that I can't hear. All I can hope is these worthless puddles of melted Popsicle will evaporate soon, and no one will know I was ever here.

"Yes, a half hour will be fine. Thank you."

Principal Sullivan hangs up. "You can go wait in the nurse's office until your mom comes."

She doesn't look at me. She doesn't have to. Because I'm not there. I've evaporated up. Leaving nothing in my wake—nothing except an oddly sticky chair.

▲ ● ■

I don't see my mom when she comes to drop off a shirt for me. All I know is that when they call me down from the nurse's office, the yellow alligator shirt that Grandma Agnes sent me after her trip to the Everglades is folded neatly on the secretary's desk. It's only when I open the shirt that I discover the note inside.

Don't ever do this again.

After I've changed into the new shirt in the bathroom, I tuck the note in my pocket. It won't happen again.

Not ever.

Chapter 27

MY MOM'S EYES ARE STONY WHEN SHE COMES HOME from work. She drops her bag and sinks down into her chair at the kitchen table. Then she closes her eyes and rests her head in her hands.

"I'm so sorry," I say. "I wasn't thinking."

"No, you weren't."

"Did you get in trouble at work?"

She lifts her head to eye me. "Yes. And I don't understand why you'd do something like that."

She hasn't seen the shirt, I remind myself. She's just talking about the dress code.

"I didn't realize tank tops weren't allowed," I say.

My mom closes her eyes. "Because your straps were showing?"

"They weren't."

"Then what was the problem?"

I stare down at the table. "Principal Sullivan said my shoulders were distracting."

My mom lets out a long breath. "I had to leave work because your shoulders were showing?" She rubs her face with her hands. "What could possibly be so wrong with your shoulders that they have to be covered at all times? Let me see the shirt."

I freeze. "Mom, I don't think—"

"Because if it's one of those skimpy kinds, then maybe I'd understand."

I shake my head at lightning speed. "It's not. I promise!"

My mom fixes her eyes on me. "Then, show me."

I take a deep breath and reach into my backpack to pull out the tank top, still balled up from school.

She takes it from me, opening it up as she does. "This is just a regular tank top! These straps are plenty thick. What a ridiculous rule. Do your shoulders even . . ." She pauses. She is reading. She is reading the words GOD IS A WOMAN.

"Agnes." Her voice is quiet. Shaking. "Why on earth would you wear something like this to the school where my boss's daughter goes—a shirt he would find so deeply offensive . . ." She swallows. "I can't talk to you right now." She stands up. "I'm sorry."

"Mom—"

But she's already disappeared into her bedroom, closing the door behind her.

I sink into my chair. Then I ball the tank top back up and throw it into the trash.

I should have just told her it was skimpy.

I have dinner made and on the table when my mom comes through the door after work the next night. Tomato soup with peanut butter toast on the side. No way am I also going to be responsible for being late to confirmation class this week.

When it's time for her to drive me she doesn't say anything the whole ride.

"I'm sorry about yesterday, Mom," I say as she pulls into a church parking space.

She presses her lips together and taps the clock on the dashboard. "Don't be late" is all she says.

I'm not late. I arrive at the pastor's parlor even before Pastor Paul. Miranda and Tya are already there, laughing about something their coach said at practice.

Or at least they were until Miranda sees me. "Why are you even here?" Miranda demands.

I tuck my head. "My mom is making me and . . ." I trail off. Miranda's looking at me like I'm mud.

"This is all a joke to you, isn't it?" Miranda continues. "*We're* all a joke to you."

I shake my head, but no words come out. What could I possibly say that won't make her even more upset at me? It's like I've frozen up again. Now I'm a Popsicle of mud.

"Is God a joke to you, too?" she asks.

"No," I say. "It's not like that." But it's too little, too late.

Miranda nudges her chair to face away from mine as Pastor Paul and Jaclyn arrive.

Pastor Paul starts in on today's lesson about the Last Supper, and I know I should be paying attention, but all I can think about is that opossum mom in the middle of the road.

When it's time to answer questions in our workbooks, I take out my opossum notebook, slip it over my workbook and start writing furiously.

THE OPINION OF AN OPOSSUM

There's a split second when your opossum life flashes before your eyes.

When you wonder if freezing up is just too dangerous a strategy.

That maybe your whole entire kind will keep getting run over again and again if you can't figure out a better way to deal with things when they get intense.

The chicken shouldn't be the only one who gets to cross the road, right?

— Chapter 28 —

I REFUSE TO STAY FROZEN IN FEAR. TO BE STUCK IN place just waiting for the next car to run me down.

When the church secretary shows up at the door and Pastor Paul has to duck out "for a few minutes," I take a deep breath and try again with Miranda.

"I don't think anyone here is a joke," I say quietly, "including God."

Miranda turns to me, her face as impenetrable as steel, but I keep going. "I want to believe in God, but no matter how much I try, I just can't get there when I picture God looking like that." I gesture to the picture above the bookcase that shows God as an old man with a long white beard.

Miranda's eyes bulge, wide as headlights. "But that's what He's supposed to look like!"

"Not for me—" I start, but then I falter. The benefit of staying silent is that you don't dig that muddy hole even bigger for your muddy self.

"Why should YOU get to decide God looks different than what the church thinks?" Miranda cries.

I consider this. "Because I'm the one trying to believe."

"But that's not how it works!" Miranda says. She turns to Tya for support, but Tya is looking at me, not at her, her expression unreadable.

"So how do you picture God?" says a voice. I turn to find Jaclyn looking at me with more interest than I've ever seen her show.

Jaclyn is asking me a question? And not in a sarcastic way? Like she actually cares about the answer.

"For me," I say, keeping my eyes on Jaclyn so I don't have to look at Miranda, "I think it'd be easier to believe if I imagine God looking like . . ." I pause and collect my courage. "Like Maya Angelou."

The room goes silent.

Are they just as blown away as I am? Are they all imagining God as looking like Maya Angelou? Regal, unapologetic, and unshakably calm.

Then Jaclyn cuts through my thoughts. "I don't have a clue who that is."

So I guess they're not quite as blown away as I was—which makes sense because it's not like I knew who Maya Angelou was a few weeks ago either.

"She was an author and a poet," I say. "And a dancer and a singer and an activist . . ." I stop. Miranda is glaring at me.

I try to steady my breathing and say, "I just think that people should be allowed to picture God any way they want." Saying this aloud makes it all the more clear, and I add, "Especially if it helps them believe."

"That's blasphemy," Miranda hisses. "If someone wants to believe in God, all they have to do is pray and read the Bible and listen to people like Pastor Paul. Who, I should mention, will be here any minute and certainly won't approve of this conversation."

"Why Maya Angelou?" Tya asks.

"Don't encourage her," Miranda says, but Tya ignores her and waits for me to answer.

"Because she was wise and had a huge heart and stood up for the underdog," I say. "But it doesn't have to be her. There are lots of other people who are inspiring. Like Harriet Tubman. And that woman who planted millions of trees in Kenya. And Jane Goodall—and honestly, Jesus, too! I mean, why do we only talk about Jesus's birth and death and how he died for our sins? Why don't we spend more time talking about how he lived his life?!" I realize my voice is rising, and I try to dial it back. "Anyway. It doesn't have to be Maya Angelou, but when she speaks, I feel like she's speaking right to me."

"If you don't stop talking about this, I'll—" Miranda cries.

But Tya cuts her off, looking at me. "Even though you haven't faced the kind of struggles Maya Angelou faced?"

I glance between Miranda and Tya. "I guess I want to look to someone stronger than me—and wiser—to help get me over my own stuff. But I know it's different stuff."

Tya opens her mouth to say something just as Miranda yelps, "Pastor Paul! I'm so glad you're back!"

"Sorry that took a bit!" Pastor Paul says. "Let's get back to the workbook now, shall we?"

I sneak a glance at Miranda. Everything about her is tight: her lips, her forehead, her hands clenched together. Like she's about to burst.

If Miranda hadn't told her dad before, she will now.

Maya Angelou said to tell the truth, and I just did. But I wish I knew how to do it without feeling so rattled.

Chapter 29

AFTER EVERYTHING THAT'S HAPPENED, I FEEL I NEED TO
talk to Gracy, so I head over to her house.

"Are you okay?" Gracy says as soon as she opens the door.

"Yeah," I lie.

"Is that true?"

I study her floor mat. "My mom's upset with me."

"Does she have reason to be?"

I nod. "I messed up. I wore this tank top to school, and
there's a dress code and . . . it's complicated . . ." I trail off.

"Come in," Gracy says. "I've got to get to my anthropology
club meeting soon, but we can chat while I pack my dinner."

In the kitchen she gestures to a chair, and I perch on the
edge of it as she starts slicing a pear. "When I was young, girls
weren't allowed to wear pants to school," she tells me. "Not
even in the cold. Do you know how miserable that was?"

I picture my mom in her skirts on cold winter mornings,
shivering as she waits for the car's heat to kick in. I nod. "My

mom's boss makes her wear stockings even though it's not like an official rule . . ."

"That kind of understood expectation can be even worse than a rule—when there's nothing in writing you can push against."

"Yeah, and my mom can't wait to take them off the minute she gets home."

"I get that!" Gracy laughs. "You know, one of my first research papers in college was about the role of pants in power dynamics."

"You wrote a paper on pants?"

Gracy smiles. "That's what you get to do when you're a sociology and anthropology major."

"Well, I guess I should be happy I don't have to wear skirts all the time."

Gracy nods. "But just because things aren't as bad as they used to be doesn't mean you can't expect them to be better. The only way change happens is if we keep pushing for it year after year. Unraveling centuries of misguided assumptions takes lots of work."

"That makes sense," I say. "And even Jesus didn't wear pants back in the day. All the pictures show him in flowing robes."

"Well, don't forget that the pictures you're seeing are just an artist's interpretation and most of them are probably wrong. For example, Jesus was Middle Eastern, so chances are he wouldn't have the pale skin American and European artists like to give him."

While I'm pondering this, Gracy starts looking in her cupboard for a container to hold her salad. "I can never find my reusable containers," she mutters. "I must have left one at the last meeting. Ah, there's one."

Gracy smiles at me. "Now where were we? Tell me about your tank top."

I take a deep breath. "The school rule against them is ridiculous, but the problem wasn't just that I was wearing a tank top. It was also what the tank top said. Because it's probably going to get my mom in trouble at work, and then she won't get the promotion she needs to pay off our credit card bill and—"

Gracy raises her eyebrows. "That's a lot of pressure on the words of one little shirt."

"Well, they weren't just any words." I pause. "It said 'God is a Woman.'"

Gracy's eyebrows shoot even higher. But then her whole face shifts, and I realize she's biting back a smile. "I'm sorry," she says. "I imagine this is all quite complicated and difficult for you, but—" Her smile takes over. "Still. That took guts."

"Thanks . . . it *is* all pretty confusing. I just don't understand why I'm supposed to believe in that angry God from the Old Testament or even just in a God that's an old man with a long beard?"

"Well, ultimately it will be up to you what you choose to believe in," Gracy says. "We can talk more tomorrow when I take you to the orthodontist."

She picks up her keys, and as we walk outside, she stops and looks at me for a moment. "It's good you're asking questions,

Agnes. And don't forget that the men interpreting the words of the prophets often had their own agendas."

"What are you saying?"

"That their opinions affected their writing. And they had a lot of opinions! But you get to have opinions, too. And yours are just as important."

— Chapter 30 —

WHEN MY MOM GETS HOME, SHE POKES HER HEAD IN my room. "Agnes, can I come in?"

I nod, and she takes a seat next to me on the bed. "I shouldn't have stopped talking to you," she says. "I don't want you to think that I'm mad at you."

"Wait." I sit up. "You're not?"

"No. I'm angry with myself and I'm—"

"With yourself? Really?"

"Yes. And I'm angry at the situation," she continues. "I'm angry that my shot at a promotion isn't about my ability to do my job. I'm angry that my boss would care what my daughter wears. But mostly . . ." She swallows. "I'm angry that I haven't had the guts to say what I think."

I open my mouth, but no words come out.

"The longer you go without saying what you think, the harder it is to remember your thoughts don't have to be the same as those around you. That happened to me," she says quietly. "And now I'm letting it start to happen to you, too. That's why I'm angry." She looks at me. "I'm sorry."

I swallow the lump that's formed in my throat. "You don't have to be sorry for being angry. Some things are worth being angry about." I let out a long breath. "I'm angry, too."

"At me?" she asks.

"No," I say, and I realize that's the truth. "I'm angry about all of the things you said, too. The situation."

She nods and pulls me in close. "I wish I knew what to do."

I lean my head against her shoulder and let her rub my back. "Are there other banks where you could work?" I ask.

"Maybe. I can look into it, but it's hard to give up a good job with health insurance when you're a single parent . . ."

I pick up my head. "But is it really a good job? Can't you at least look to see if there are openings somewhere else?"

She presses her lips together and nods. "Okay."

"Thank you," I say. "There's something else, too."

"What?"

"I want to get that tank top out of the kitchen trash."

Her eyes go wide. "You threw it out?"

I nod.

She grimaces. "I dumped a whole bunch of coffee grounds in there just now."

I shrug. "So now it says what I think and smells like you."

My mom laughs and pulls me up. "Come on. I'll wash it for you. I needed to do a load of laundry anyway."

— *Chapter 31* —

WHEN GRACY PICKS ME UP FOR MY ORTHODONTIST appointment, she hands me a giant book.

"I thought you might appreciate a little historical context on dress codes," she says.

I eye the book. It's called *Essays from the First Three Centuries.* A *little* historical context?

When we arrive at the waiting room, she says, "Check out Tertullian's essay. Page 273 if I remember correctly."

Gracy sure does remember correctly, and I find the essay. It's short but hard to make sense of. "What's he saying?" I ask Gracy.

She leans over and runs her fingers along each of the lines of text in turn, putting each one into words I understand.

If you are female, then you are Eve.

You are guilty.

You are the gateway to the devil.

So don't you dare think about wearing something that makes you beautiful!

"I don't agree with this," I say. My voice is loud and clear. An older boy sitting across from me looks over, but I don't care.

"Of course you don't agree," Gracy says. "I wanted you to see how an influential interpreter of the Bible felt free to express his opinions about how women should dress. And as hard as it is to believe, writings like this have shaped a lot of our culture today."

"Eve sure gets a bad rap, doesn't she? Like she gets blamed for starting the whole world of sin."

"Her story has certainly taken on an outsize significance ever since St. Augustine developed the concept of original sin around the year 400."

"Wait! Original sin isn't in the Bible?"

"No," Gracy says. "But St. Augustine thought it was a good way to show why humans deserved to suffer. And plenty of people agreed about who to blame for it. But that's *an* interpretation. That's their *opinion*."

When the orthodontist calls me in, I barely pay attention as he works and gives me a play-by-play of some baseball game. Because I realize why Gracy wanted me to see Tertullian's writing. So I could know what I was running from. What I was up against. She wanted me to see it for what it is, a piece of an invisible web that's pulling at me, trying to get me to curl in on myself—that in this moment is finally visible.

I love how the stuff I've been learning from Gracy keeps blowing my mind. I feel like I'm at that moment in a chase where you realize you've had it. That it's time to straighten up tall and stand your ground. When what's been chasing you now needs to run.

And there's something powerful about saying "I don't agree with this" out loud—about something printed in a *book*. Ideas printed in so many books!

Fifteen minutes later, the orthodontist taps my teeth. "You know, those sharp teeth of yours are starting to align."

Even with all that stuff in my mouth, I smile.

Chapter 32

TYA AND I BOTH GET DROPPED OFF AT CONFIRMATION class at the same time. Her dad waves to her enthusiastically from the car. "I'll pick you up when it's over, Tyborg."

Tya rolls her eyes and smiles back at him.

"Tyborg like cyborg," she explains as we go through the door. "It turns out if you like robots when you're three, you get stuck with a weird family nickname forever."

"That's pretty awesome," I say. I'm relieved she doesn't seem upset with me. I also kind of wish I had a family that made up cool nicknames for one another.

I sneak a peek at Tya as we walk down the hallway past the church kitchen. "Do you think I'm wrong to picture God as Maya Angelou?"

Tya looks at me and shrugs. "No. I think it's kind of cool. My dad likes to read poems to us after dinner, and I always love when he reads hers."

I nod and say, "Cool" back to her. We walk down the rest of

the hall in silence, but I feel so much lighter on my feet that it's almost like I'm flying.

Except that when we near the pastor's parlor, I spot Miranda, and Tya brings me back down to earth. "You know, of course Miranda won't agree, but what can you do?"

Before we can even sit, Pastor Paul rushes in and flips on the light. "Good. You're all here," he says. "I need a favor. There's a parishioner who needs help this evening, and I have to talk with her now." He tries to catch his breath. "I'm very sorry, but could you do the reading in the workbook without me for a bit?"

"Of course," Miranda says. "We'll start it right away. Don't worry about us."

Pastor Paul smiles. "I knew I could count on you girls. Miranda, you're in charge. I promise I'll be back as soon as I can."

"We'll make sure we read it carefully," Miranda calls after him as he disappears down the hall.

I take out my workbook and start in on the reading. I look up when someone nudges me with their sneaker. It's Jaclyn. "Hey," she says, "What was the name of that poet lady again?"

"Maya Angelou," I say quietly.

"What kind of poems did she write?" Jaclyn asks, not exactly quietly.

"Uh . . ." I mumble. Miranda is glaring at both of us.

"You should show her the video of Maya reading 'Still I Rise,'" Tya says without looking up from the reading.

114

I dig into my bag for my phone, quickly pull up the video, and pass it over to Jaclyn. "Here."

Maya's low, gravelly voice fills the room, each of her words taking up its own space and time. Jaclyn watches, riveted . . . *You may write me down in history, with your bitter, twisted lies . . .*

And even though I've read and listened to the poem many times before, it's different listening to it with other people.

Jaclyn has pulled the phone so close to her that it's like she's having a private video chat. With her free hand, she's holding on tight to one of the knots in her hoodie drawstring like if she lets go Maya will stop talking, and that can't happen.

But then I look at Miranda. She is pale, and her eyes are on the phone, full of fear. "You all are supposed to be working," she says. "You're going to get us in trouble!"

And suddenly, all I can see is her outside the auditorium at school, her head bowed, following her dad to the car.

"And we're supposed to be studying God here," Miranda hisses. "Enough of this!" She grabs the phone out of Jaclyn's hand. "This is church!"

"That's exactly what I was about to say." Pastor Paul's voice cuts through the room. "Even if you've finished with the reading," he says, moving quickly into the room, "this is not a time to take out your phones and watch videos on them."

"Pastor Paul," Miranda stammers. "I didn't . . . I tried to . . ."

Pastor Paul waves her off and moves back into his spot at the head of the table. "Let's just put the phone away, and you can all make it up to me by knowing the correct answers about this reading."

Miranda's lips quiver like she's going to cry. She flings the phone onto my bag and sinks down into her seat.

And then I realize: Miranda never turned the video off. There is Maya's voice, strong and sure.

I rise.

I rise.

I rise.

Chapter 33

I'M BRUSHING MY TEETH WHEN MY PHONE BUZZES. IT'S a text from Miranda. I never get texts from Miranda—unless she's doing "the Christian thing" each year and inviting me to her birthday party.

No false prophets, she texts. Remember??

Is she going to tell her dad about me? Has she already told him? I spit out my toothpaste and hustle into my bedroom.

I know, I quickly type. This is different.

You shall have no other gods, Miranda texts. That's the 1st commandment. Before not killing.

I'm not talking about multiple gods, I write back. Just multiple ways to think about God.

Idk . . . Miranda writes. is that really different?

Yes, it's different. God shows up in so many different forms throughout the Bible. No one says the burning bush was a false prophet. And aren't people allowed to believe in other religions if they want to? Aren't those people our neighbors, and didn't Jesus say to love our neighbors?

I'm about to write that when Miranda texts again:

You're letting yourself get deceived. Like Eve.

I let out a long breath. Why does everything always have to
end up back with Eve?
I text her back:

You're right. I don't want to be deceived like Eve. I don't
want to believe lies.

But what if the lie is that there's something wrong with us
just because we're girls?

That we should never stop apologizing for that. What if
that's not true? Did you know original sin isn't even in the
Bible? It's someone's opinion. And we're allowed to dis-
agree with it.

I flop down on my bed and watch as she reads it but doesn't
respond. I wait for a while before giving up. But as I turn off my
phone for the night, I realize something. I told the truth—my
truth. And I'm not rattled this time. I feel good.

Chapter 34

FOR THE PAST WEEK I'VE BEEN EATING LUNCH IN THE library, but today I stay in the cafeteria after getting my food.

I sit down with my tray across from Mo. "I'm ready to stop avoiding you."

He swallows and nods. "Eight days is a long time to go without your best friend." He pokes at the foil lid he pulled off his yogurt. "But I deserved it. I'm really sorry."

I stare at my tray. "I know."

"But I want to tell you why I'm sorry," Mo says. "I didn't think the tank top idea through. I still don't get why the school would act like shoulders are bare butts, but I should have realized they might." He takes a breath. "And I'm really sorry that I didn't come to school that day. I know we had a deal and everything, but . . ." He drops his head.

"But what?"

"But I was scared. Every time I thought about going up on that stage and reading that shopping cart story, I felt like I was

119

going to throw up." He pokes more at his yogurt lid. "I did throw up. That's why my mom let me stay home."

"You actually threw up?"

"I know. Stupid, right? I'm not supposed to be scared like that."

That word *supposed to* sticks at me.

"Says who?" I say.

Mo jabs another hole in the yogurt lid. "I'm just not."

"But why not?" I say. "What makes you think that?"

"What are you talking about?"

"You know how people always say it's bad for boys to be weak or to be scared?" I say. "Who decided that anyway?"

Mo lets out a long breath. "Well, they're probably right."

"Not if they're the ones saying my shoulders are a distraction." I stop cutting my chicken parmesan. "I may be just one person"—I lean forward onto my elbows—"but I think you're allowed to be as scared as you want to be."

"Thanks," Mo says. "You know, I was really convinced I didn't care about opopinions . . . but somehow the thought of opopinions about what I wrote felt different."

Just then someone taps the microphone at the front of the cafeteria for a student council announcement about the talent show.

When they're done, Mo looks at me. "So how'd you get all wisdom-y?"

I shrug. "Gracy's been teaching me stuff."

"So you're not mad?"

I shake my head. "Not at you. Not anymore, at least. I'm still mad at a whole lot of other stuff." Then I realize I sound just like my mom. But this time it's in a good way.

He nods. "I'm mad at everyone who thinks shoulders are bare butts."

"Thanks." I give him a fist bump. "It helps to share the burden."

He reaches into his lunch bag. "I know it doesn't really make up for anything, but . . ." He slides his thinly sliced apple over to me. "You can have all of these today."

If the apple in the Garden of Eden had been thinly sliced, it'd have been even more impossible to resist.

"Thank you." I push them back into the center of the table. "But we can share them."

Together we eat every single one of those apple slices, and they are like a crisp, fresh new day.

Chapter 35

AS SOON AS MY MOM GETS HOME, SHE CALLS ME INTO the kitchen. She doesn't even take her skirt and stockings off first.

"Sit down," she tells me.

I sit.

"Mr. Adams called me into his office today and asked me some . . . questions."

I try to stay calm. Maybe this has nothing to do with Miranda.

"He asked if I had taught you the Ten Commandments. If you knew the first commandment about only having one God."

Or maybe this conversation has everything to do with her. I stare at the crack on the kitchen table.

"He asked if I knew you were behaving sinfully and that he's not sure 'my family values align with the values of the bank.'" My mom swallows. "Agnes, did Miranda see you in that tank top?"

I nod. "And I may have talked about it all with her, too."

"Agnes . . ." My mom's voice is so tired.

"I just tried to explain that I thought there could be multiple ways to think about God," I say quickly. I keep my eyes on the table. "I wanted her to be more open-minded. I guess it didn't work."

When she doesn't say anything, I sneak a look at her. Her mouth is closed tight. Like words are battling to get out, but she's not going to let them.

"Mom," I say. "I'm sorry. But you shouldn't feel guilty. Remember? You agreed that the situation with Mr. Adams is unfair."

"I did. I do." She rubs her temples. "But he sure loves lording that promotion over me." She sighs and then pushes her chair back. "I know what we need."

I have no idea what to expect, but it certainly wasn't her reappearing with a pile of books.

"Poetry," my mom says as she deposits them on the table. "When you started talking about Maya Angelou, it made me remember how much I used to love poetry. It helped give me strength after your dad died. I can't believe I haven't read these for so long."

I eye the poets. Mary Oliver. Rumi. Edna St. Vincent Millay.

"I needed strength then," she says. "Maybe they'll give us the strength we need now."

I think of how those simple words of Maya Angelou opened up something inside me that I hadn't known was there. I squeeze my mom's hand and then reach for the book closest to me, Mary Oliver. I open it to a random page. And there, waiting for me, is a question.

Do you bow your head when you pray or do you look up into that blue space?

Take your choice, prayers fly from all directions.

I pull the book closer to me and turn to another page . . .

Prayers that are made out of grass

I've stopped breathing.

How did I not know this kind of writing existed?

Together, my mom and I spend the rest of the evening reading poetry.

And even though I know none of this will change anything with Mr. Adams—that my mom will still have to wear uncomfortable stockings and worry about what he thinks—for right now he has no power to lord anything over us.

— Chapter 36 —

ON SATURDAY MORNING, I ARRIVE AT GRACY'S DOORSTEP. When she doesn't answer the door, I go looking for her and find her around back working in her garden.

"Beautiful morning, isn't it, Agnes?" she says as soon as she sees me. There's a plant lying on the ground next to her, its roots exposed, waiting to be transplanted.

"Gracy, I have a question. How are you supposed to change when you're surrounded by people who don't want anything to change?"

She unearths a rock and picks it up. "Ah yes, change can be hard. I've been thinking about your tank top and the attitudes toward women. You know it was only a little over a hundred years ago that women got the right to vote?"

"I guess that is pretty recent?"

Gracy laughs. "Yes, change is extremely hard, especially when you're talking about breaking down beliefs that have been held for a long, long time. Do you know much about Paul?" she asks.

At first, I think she's talking about Pastor Paul, but then I realize she's talking about Paul from the Bible. "Not all that much," I say.

"Paul was a devout follower of Jesus," she says. "He believed in everything Jesus preached, including that men and women were equal. But you can believe something at face value, and at the same time your gut will tell you the opposite. Paul had grown up in a world where women weren't treated equally, and it's hard not to be affected by that."

I think of Mo. His gut told him he wasn't supposed to be scared.

"So when women were asking lots of questions at church meetings, Paul supposedly wrote that they should stay silent," Gracy continues. "It's not even clear if those were his words or a note in the margin from a scribe. But regardless, there was a whole host of people ready to turn it into doctrine."

I feel my breath catch. "And then it gets written into the Bible."

"And incorporated into the culture," Gracy says.

I sink down into the grass, next to the plant waiting to be transplanted. "One person can really shape things that much?"

Then she picks up the transplant, cradling it by the roots. "Culture shapes us and we shape culture. It's just a matter of which one is stronger."

I watch Gracy gently place the roots in the hole. "You know what Paul wrote in a letter to one of the early churches? He wrote that love rejoices in the truth." She begins to fill the hole up with dirt. "I like to hope that when we have the courage to speak the truth, it'll be met with love."

I eye Gracy's compost bin. "But what if it's not? And what if nothing ever changes?"

Gracy sits down in the grass next to me. "Change is a long process. That defensiveness we feel when we're forced to see things in a new way? That feeling is the waking."

I look at her. Her eyes are bright.

"Just think of all the worms under this dirt." She gestures to the garden. "They aerate the soil so that plants like this can grow. They can't see the effects of all their work—they don't even have eyes—but that doesn't stop them. One little bit at a time, they transform the ground we live on." She gives me a mischievous grin. "And for all the rules the neighborhood association has about plants and animals, they don't have a single one about worms."

She plucks a flower from a plant just like the one she just transplanted and hands it to me. "It's a nasturtium, and it's edible. Try it."

I finger its delicate orange petals. I've never heard of an edible flower, but I do what Gracy says and put it in my mouth.

She watches me as I chew.

"Doesn't it taste like fresh morning dew?" she says.

It's like having springtime burst forth inside my mouth.

I smile. "Yes, it does."

THE OPINION OF AN OPOSSUM

Maybe I almost died.
    But in the end, I didn't. (So I guess it wasn't the end!)
    What happens next is what matters most.
    Because then I can stand back up. And keep surviving.
    One day at a time.

Chapter 37

AS USUAL, MIRANDA'S ALREADY AT CONFIRMATION CLASS when I arrive, and is sitting in the dark. I guess I could be angry that she told her dad, but mostly when I see her like this, I feel sad. I turn on the light and sit as far from her as possible.

Tya gets there soon after. She nods to me, then she and Miranda start talking about the lacrosse game.

"Agnes."

I look up to see Jaclyn. "Can you remind me of the name of that poem you played last week? And does she have other videos?"

"'Still I Rise,'" Tya says. "And she has a ton of great poems."

"Cool," Jaclyn says. I glance up to see that she's actually writing that down in a notebook. I didn't know Jaclyn had a notebook.

When she's done, Jaclyn looks up at me. "I gotta tell you, your idea of picturing God as looking like her has blown my mind."

I suck in my breath just as Miranda leans forward. "Don't

be talking about that stuff again!" She looks to Tya, her eyes pleading. "Pastor Paul'll be here any minute!"

"He's not here yet," Jaclyn snaps. She stashes her notebook away. "And we should be able to talk about this if we want to."

Miranda shakes her head quickly. "This isn't an okay place to question what God looks like."

"Says who?" Jaclyn says. "If I want to picture God looking the same way Agnes does, you don't get to stop me."

Miranda has shrunk into herself. "But it's not right."

"It's okay, Miranda," I say. "Other people are allowed to believe in different religions, aren't they? You might even believe in a different one if you were born to a different family. So maybe there isn't just *one* right way. And we're free to choose."

"But we're here in *this* church." Miranda looks down. "You know, my aunt says one of the secret powers of a woman is the ability to put our own needs aside so that we can do what's right for the people around us."

I think about what Miranda is saying for a moment. What is it that makes us believe we have to stop ourselves from saying what we think? Who benefits from us bottling up our thoughts?

"But at least when you question stuff aloud, it lets other people know they're not alone," Jaclyn says. She's started tying knots in her hoodie drawstring again and keeps her eyes on the knots. "When you said that stuff about God last week, Agnes,"—she glances up at me—"I felt better, because I think more like you do."

I bite my lip. "How do you picture God?"

Jaclyn pulls her hoodie up until her face almost disappears.

"I guess I like to think of God as always around. Listening. Watching. I don't picture God as a person, though. More like light. Like the way light can make everything it touches a little better. A little easier." She releases her tightened hood and fingers the line of knots on the drawstring. "My favorite part of church is when they light the candle and there's new light. When I tie a knot, I imagine that I'm lighting a candle, too. It helps me."

I realize I've stopped breathing. I've never thought about those knots as anything more than a weird habit.

Tya's fingers twitch toward Jaclyn's sweatshirt. "All those candles," she says.

Jaclyn studies all of the knots. "Yeah, there are a lot of them, aren't there? Well, sometimes things at home are kind of . . . dark." She swallows and looks up at Tya. "How do you picture God?"

Tya glances at Miranda. "I don't picture a specific thing. I've just always done what my grandmother does. In my head, I replace the word God with the word *love*."

"You what?" Miranda says.

"I've never ever thought of doing that," I say, "but I like it." I imagine this whole force of love sweeping through the room. It would be full of light, just like Jaclyn imagines, too. "It feels amazing," I continue. "And this is why we need to share, because otherwise . . . because otherwise everyone feels like THEY'RE COMPLETELY IN THE DARK!"

I realize I'm shouting at the exact moment that the door opens and Pastor Paul walks in.

"You're all here already!" he says. "Girls are so good at being on time. And look, you've already got the light on and everything."

We sure do. It's like every single light in this room is blazing bright.

— Chapter 38 —

WHEN CONFIRMATION CLASS IS OVER, JACLYN AND TYA walk out together, chatting about poetry. Miranda walks out next to me, her arms folded against her chest.

"I still don't think it's good to be asking these kinds of questions," she says.

"It is," I say. "It can be freeing."

"There's nothing freeing about saying things aloud that should stay unsaid," she mutters. "It's dangerous."

"You're the one who told your dad," I blurt.

Miranda stops and faces me. "Told my dad what?"

"That I'm like a heretic or something. My mom's been in line to get a promotion, but now your dad—her boss—is worried that she hasn't taught her daughter the commandments. I'm pretty sure she won't be getting that promotion now."

Miranda's face has gone red. Redder than I've ever seen it.

"I get it," I say. "You told him what I said. I mean, he's your dad and all."

"But I didn't tell him," Miranda says.

"It's okay." I start walking. "I'm not even angry about it, really. It is what it is."

Miranda is shaking. "But I didn't tell him, Agnes! He must have . . ." She squeezes her eyes shut. "He must be reading my diary. Because that's exactly what I wrote. That I was worried what you were talking about went against the commandments. I even deleted our texts because I know sometimes he reads those, but I didn't think he'd read my diary! And that's why he knew to show up to see the talent show audition, too, because I'd written I was excited to do the dance I'd been practicing. Oh wow, and now that I think about it, that must be why he sat me down the other night and lectured me about the importance of taking the Bible seriously and not letting other interpretations cloud my faith." Miranda swallows and looks at me. "Because I had written that I thought you might have a point. I mean, just maybe. Not that I agree with you or anything, but . . ." She stops for a minute to gather her thoughts. "See? This is why these things shouldn't be allowed out in words."

"But it's not healthy to bottle it up either," I say.

I look at her. There are tears in her eyes.

"I'm so sorry about your mom. If she doesn't get a promotion, it's all because of me."

"No, it isn't, Miranda. You should be allowed to think about things . . . for yourself. That's not something you should blame yourself for."

"Then who am I supposed to blame?"

I shake my head. "Not us."

── Chapter 39 ──

THE NEXT WEDNESDAY WHEN I GET OFF AT MY BUS STOP, I do a double take. My mom's car is in the driveway.

My stomach drops.

She's not supposed to be home from work for another two hours. She couldn't have lost her job, right? Not getting the promotion was going to be bad enough, but . . . I can't think about what no job would mean.

I rush inside to find her lying on the couch. "What are you doing?" I say. "Are you okay?"

"I'm fine." She sits up to make a space for me to sit. "I was just resting my eyes."

"But why aren't you at work? Did you—"

She cuts me off. "I called in sick," she says.

"Oh." I look at her. She's never sick, so I don't know what Sick Mom looks like. Maybe not that different from Regular Mom.

"But I'm not sick," she says.

My eyebrows shoot up. "You lied?"

135

Her eyebrows go up, too. "It was for a good cause."

Then I see it. A smile starting to form on her lips.

"What?" I say. "What'd you do?"

The smile takes over her face. "I interviewed for a job at a different bank."

"You did! How'd it go? Which bank? Did you get the job???"

She laughs. "I don't know yet, but the interview went well, and they said they'd call by the end of the day. They just lost a teller, and they're understaffed right now. It's a little farther away, on the far side of town, but the pay is better."

"That's great!"

She winks at me. "That's what I thought. And I'd rather drive an extra fifteen minutes each way . . . if it means you get to say what you believe."

I feel my breath catch in my throat, and I throw my arms around her with so much force that the two of us topple over onto the couch.

Her head is smushed between two pillows, and after she stops laughing, she closes her eyes and takes a deep breath, and I rest my head against her.

She runs her hand through my hair. "If someone had told me when you were born how much I was going to learn from you, I wouldn't have believed it."

I can hear her heartbeat, and I slow my breathing until each inhale and exhale stretches across three lub-dubs.

We lie there together, just breathing, until her phone rings.

She sits up. I sit up and I lean in to hear as much as I can.

"Yes, thank you," my mom is saying. "I enjoyed meeting you, too."

I wait for her to say something. *Please let this work.*

Because really, who wouldn't want to hire my mom?

Finally, her expression changes, and that big smile is back. "Oh, that's wonderful," she says. "Yes, that works for me."

When she hangs up, she lets out a "WHOOP!" and flops back onto the couch. "We did it. I can't wait to give my notice at work." She looks at me. "It's such a relief, but, gosh, that was hard."

I swallow. "Gracy says that change is hard because even if you believe something needs to change on the surface, it's what's in your bones that wins out."

"Gracy is right about a lot of things," Mom says. "But in this case, it was the stuff on the surface keeping me from changing—all those people who said, 'you're a single parent with a good job—don't mess with it.' And you know what was deep in my bones?" She nudges my leg. "My love for you. That's what helped me most."

I grin and nudge her right back.

"You ready for a celebratory dinner?" she says. "I'm thinking ravioli and ice cream."

I stand up. "You get to stay on the couch. I'll get it ready."

I'm in the kitchen when Mom calls to me from the couch. "Agnes," she says, "do you know what this means? It means that you don't have to go to confirmation class anymore."

"Really? What about Grandma Agnes?"

"I can talk to her. She'll be upset with me anyway, not you, and I'm okay with that."

I let out a long breath. "I'll think about it."

But I only have to think about it for a minute and picture Jaclyn, Tya, and even Miranda. There's no way I'm skipping out on them.

— Chapter 40 —

MIRANDA IS ALREADY THERE WHEN I GET TO THE pastor's parlor, perched on the edge of her chair.

"Miranda!" I say. "You turned the lights on!"

"I figured no one said we aren't allowed to get here early, right?" she says quickly. "And if we're here, there should probably be light?" She looks around like Pastor Paul might pop out of a wall any second to tell her she's wrong.

And when Pastor Paul's head does pop in—through a doorway—all he does is apologize. "I'm so sorry, but I'm going to have to be late to our meeting again to deal with some spring festival preparations. Please just keep yourselves occupied until I'm back."

He doesn't even wait for us to answer before he's disappeared down the hall.

Tya and Jaclyn show up soon after. "You know, I think we need a plan," Jaclyn says as soon as she sits down.

"What kind of plan?" Tya asks.

"I don't know," Jaclyn says. "All I know is that the last few times, I came home from confirmation class feeling good."

Miranda makes some kind of animal sound. Like a whimper.

Tya turns to her. "Are you okay? Gosh, you look like you're going to be sick."

Miranda shakes her head. She's staring down at her lap. "You all have to promise not to tell."

We all promise, and then she says in a whisper, "I've been lying! It's a sin. I know it is. But . . ."

"What have you lied about?" I ask.

"Is it about how you picture God?" Jaclyn asks.

Miranda's eyes get wide. "No! It's not that." She looks between us. "I really do like imagining God as looking like an older man. It feels comfortable. No, it's . . ." She takes a deep breath. "It's my diary." She tells Jaclyn about what she discovered. Tya must already know because she nods along as Miranda explains. "But now that I know that my dad is reading it . . ." Miranda looks at each of us. "I started writing things that aren't true! Things that I know he'll want to hear."

I suck in my breath.

Jaclyn breaks out in a big smile. "That's awesome. Two can play his game. What have you written?"

"That I'm going to sing the song in the talent show just the way he wants, without dancing at all," Miranda whispers. "Do you think that's an okay thing to lie about?" She looks at me. "Like if sometimes you don't need everyone to know the truth? If it's enough that you yourself know?"

"Maybe," I say, glancing at the others, "but don't you think he's going to find out?"

Tya nods. "Yeah, there's no way your dad would miss the talent show."

Miranda grimaces. "I'm hoping to figure out some way to stop him from going, but I haven't yet. I just really want to do the dance I've been practicing to go with the song." She sighs. "Gosh, I sound ridiculous. You guys are all focused on big, serious stuff, and I'm worrying about a little talent show."

"It's not little," Tya says. "Your dream is to be up on stage singing and dancing. So you should care about that, and you should push against the people trying to keep you from it." She pauses. "The little things matter."

Miranda looks at Tya and swallows. "Thank you."

Nobody says anything for a moment, but it doesn't feel like an awkward silence. It feels . . . comfortable. And for the first time, I'm sad that this confirmation class will be coming to an end.

"How would you feel about getting together to talk about stuff like this, separate from confirmation class?" I say.

"Like talk about the stuff in our lives we're trying to figure out?" Tya says. "That'd be cool."

"Or about how to do the right thing?" Jaclyn adds. "Or at least figure out if there is a right thing. I need that."

"We can't meet at my house," Miranda says. "That's for sure."

"I'm pretty sure we could meet at mine," I say.

"Mine too," Tya says.

"It'd be different than confirmation class, though, right?" Miranda asks.

"For sure!" I say. "No workbooks for a start."

"I like it," Tya says. "How about we call ourselves the Figuring Stuff Out Group?"

"FSO Group," says Jaclyn.

"Or Figuring Out What We Believe," Tya says.

I nod. "Finding Our Own Truth Group."

"FOOT Group?" Jaclyn says. "That's cool. You stand up with your feet."

"That's good with me," says Tya.

Miranda looks at Tya and then nods. "Just tell me when to show up."

And suddenly I realize we just did what Gracy says women have been doing for thousands of years. When faced with something stressful, they come together with other women and see if they can figure it out.

— *Chapter 41* —

WHEN PASTOR PAUL ARRIVES, I LISTEN TO HIM WAX ON about the importance of a vibrant church in our lives. But I can't help thinking: If my mom isn't going to get in trouble at her job because of me speaking my mind anymore . . . what's stopping me? I raise my hand.

"Pastor Paul," I say. "I have a question."

He nods. "It's good to ask questions, Agnes. What is it?"

"What do you imagine God looks like?"

He looks startled. "Do you mean what it says in the Bible? Because there's really no one way. It does say in Genesis that God made man in His own image, so from that we can assume—"

"But why do you think the Bible says that God made *man* in His own image?" I blurt out. "Why didn't it say 'person'? Do you think God thinks that men are better than women?"

"Oh no." He chuckles. "God loves everyone equally."

"But then why does the Bible say God made man first, and that he only made a woman so that the man could have a companion?" I ask.

He smiles. "Well, someone had to come first, and the Old Testament can be a little . . ."

I can't stop myself now. "Do you think that maybe the Bible was written at a time when women weren't treated very fairly?"

"Of course the Bible is the word of God, a God who loves everyone." He tilts his head. "But Agnes, perhaps you're asking the wrong question. Maybe it's not what God looks like that matters, maybe it's about where God lives."

"He lives in our church. It's God's house, right?" Miranda volunteers, practically leaping out of her seat.

"Yes, that's what I used to think, too," Pastor Paul says, "but God is with you even when you're not at church. The most important place that God lives . . ." He points at my heart. "Is in there."

I put my hand on my heart.

Pastor Paul closes his eyes. "When you sit by the bedside of one parishioner facing death after another, you start to see how simple it really is. Love yourself, and you will love God. Love God, and you will love yourself." He pauses. "But we, as humans, struggle to imagine something so great. Something that transcends all. Something that loves us so strongly." He opens his eyes and looks straight at me. "So if it helps to imagine God in a certain way to help you feel that love, by all means, go right ahead. It's the love that's important."

His words float above me in the air. I'm barely breathing. Because I feel it. The love inside me. All around me.

Maya Angelou plus love plus light plus steadiness.

And way bigger than I can imagine.

Chapter 42

"TRUST ME, MO," I SAY AS I DRAG HIM ONTO MY BUS. "This is exactly what I need to do, and therefore, as my best friend, you need to help me do it."

We get off the bus, and I lead Mo down the street to the park until we reach our destination: the historic sheep pen.

Mo looks at me. "I thought you were pretty clear you didn't want to have anything to do with the sheep. If I remember correctly, you said . . ."

"I was wrong," I say. "I *am* descended from sheep. Do you know what makes these sheep special?"

"They're dead?"

"Yes, but they haven't always been dead." I look at the walls of the pen that once held them. "For their whole lives, they survived. They made more sheep. And those sheep survived. And you know what they'd love?"

"To not be dead?"

I hold up my finger. "They would love to know that their descendants were doing better than just surviving, that their descendants were pushing forward and thinking about things in new ways, and . . ."

"We're talking about sheep, right?"

"We're talking about creatures that for centuries have been forced to stay inside a stone enclosure barely large enough to breathe in," I say, my voice getting louder.

Mo's brow furrows. "I thought it was opossums you were into."

"The problem is"—I wave my finger in the air—"when we don't step back and see the larger picture and understand that *no* creature treated as gross or less important will be able to thrive if we don't band together and stand up for what's right!"

Mo bites back a smile. "I've really missed you, Agnes."

I drop my finger. "I've missed you, too."

"Is that the end of your declaration or is there more?"

"Oh, it's just the beginning," I say. "Prepare yourself for a dramatic reading of 'The Opinion of an Opossum.'"

Mo rubs his hands and sits on the grass. "Oh goody. I've been waiting for this."

I stand up tall, clear my throat, and read all my opossum stories. I do my best to let my opossum's anger shine through. Because sometimes you need to let yourself feel anger to remind yourself that things shouldn't stay the way they are.

Mo doesn't say anything for a while after I finish.

"Well, what'd you think?" I ask, sitting down next to him.

"I think I've misjudged opossums."

"You're not alone on that front," I say.

"And I also think that you just gave me the courage to do what I didn't think I could do."

And then he takes his notebook out of his backpack and stands up.

"Remember, it's a story," Mo says. "You may be annoyed with the main character for a while, but stay with him. It's about where he ends up."

I lean back on my elbows. "Lay it on me."

Mo starts off, and his voice shakes a little at first, but then he settles in with Steve the shopping cart, having his wild, existential thoughts. And then he starts talking about . . . how his friend didn't show up. My stomach drops out from under me a bit because I know Steve the abandoned shopping cart is Mo—and I'm the one who's done the abandoning.

I start to apologize when Mo cuts me off.

"That's not the end," he says, digging into his backpack. "I wrote the last chapter yesterday but didn't have my notebook with me." He pulls a loose piece of paper out of a notebook and waves it at me. And then he begins to read it.

THE CONCLUSION OF
THE SHOPPING CART WHO HAD BIG THOUGHTS
by Mo

As Steve watched his friend try so hard to tell the truth—to herself first and then to others—he realized that he hadn't been telling HIMSELF the truth either.

147

It was true he didn't want to carry basketball-sized cantaloupes.

It was true he loved buildings made of Jell-O.

But WAS it true that he didn't belong at the grocery store? What if it didn't matter where he was: In the canned soup aisle or shivering with the frozen food. Or even outside, hanging out with a stop sign or on the lookout for a glimpse of some ancient sheep.

What if it wasn't about finding a place to belong? It was about finding a shopping cart to belong to?

And then came his biggest thought yet: What if the shopping cart he belonged to most of all was himself?

At that moment, he took off down the sidewalk. It felt great to feel the fresh air pass through him as he bumped along at breakneck speed. He wondered what the word was for the lightness of being, for the joy of the sound and smell of potato chip leaves crunching beneath his wheels. For the feeling that HE WAS OKAY just as he was, wherever he was. No matter if he ever carried a cantaloupe again.

Then he and his big thoughts rolled forward into the sunset . . . ready for the next adventure.

When Mo sits down next to me, I realize he's shaking.

I put my arm around him. "That was awesome."

He nods and swallows, his Adam's apple bobbing up and down. "Thank you. It's a lot to say it out loud, you know? A lot of feeling there . . ."

"Yeah," I say. "I know."

He looks at me. "I haven't told you this yet, but at the last minute I submitted this to the contest."

"You did?!" I grab his shoulders. "That's incredible!"

He nods. "But they already announced the winner. It wasn't me."

"Well, it wins in my book. You should be proud of yourself, Mo. Those judges probably just weren't ready for it yet. Sometimes it takes a while before people are up for seeing things in a new way."

Mo nods. "Yeah."

I look up at the sky. It's so huge, and the clouds look like puffy puppies. Or maybe puffy opossums.

"You know what some people call that word?" I ask.

"What word?"

"The one that describes that lightness and the freshness of the air and that feeling that you're suddenly okay the way you are?" I turn to look at Mo.

"What?" He turns to look at me.

"God."

—— *Chapter 43* ——

ON FRIDAY NIGHT, MO AND I GET FRONT-ROW SEATS for the talent show so we can cheer Sadie on, and we save a few for our families.

As we wait for the show to start, I look over at Mo. He's reading the program, but more importantly, he's wearing the new T-shirt I got him, with a graphic of an overturned shopping cart, whose wheels look like wide-open eyes. Mo was right—it's amazing what you can find on the Internet.

When my mom arrives, I do a double take. She's wearing jeans—ripped ones!

"Nice outfit," I whisper as she takes her seat.

"It feels good," she whispers back. "I feel like the old new me."

She smiles and eyes my GOD IS A WOMAN tank top, on display beneath an opened button-down shirt.

The talent show begins, and Sadie is the second act. "What do you think she's going to do this time?" I whisper to Mo as the first kids run offstage.

"I'm just hoping it doesn't involve drumming on her naked

bum," he whispers back. "It was funny this morning when she was getting dressed, but it might push the limit of appropriateness for a mixed audience."

"Well, you know the thing about Sadie," I say, "once she's done something once, it won't happen again."

As Sadie walks out on the stage, Mo shouts, "Yeah, Sadie!"

"Wahoo!" I yell.

She sees us and smiles. And then the theme song from *Moana* comes on, and she's off. She leaps into the air, her arms flung high.

My breath catches.

She's wearing a bright pink shirt with ribbons safety pinned to the back like a cape, and every time she leaps, those ribbons fly along with her. Maybe she touches down at some point during the song, but it doesn't feel like it. It feels like she's soaring higher and higher.

When the song ends, we explode in applause. Mo and I stand up, and my mom and Mo's parents do, too.

Sadie smiles, bows three different ways, and then leaves the stage.

"She has no fear," I murmur as we sit back down.

"None," he says.

"Did we used to be like that?" I say.

"I think there's a good chance." He looks back up at the stage. "And if we used to be that way, we can probably find our way back to it."

I nod. "I think so—look at my mom."

Mo gives me a fist bump. "With you every step of the way."

The next act I am excited to see is Tya's. I didn't see her audition so have no idea what she'll be doing. She holds her head high as she walks out on stage and announces she's going to recite the first one hundred fifty digits of pi. And then on a screen behind Tya, one hundred fifty numbers show up, starting with 3.1415926535 and she starts reciting them . . . and keeps going. Without looking at the screen once. Through all one hundred fifty digits.

When Tya is done, I can hear Miranda congratulating her from backstage. "You did it! So great!"

Then it's Miranda's turn. I look behind me to see if I can spot her dad, and there he is. Our FOOT Group texted back and forth trying to come up with plans to stop him from coming, but apparently none of them worked.

I hope Miranda has the guts to go through with this anyway.

I turn back around to find her standing smack in the middle of the stage with a look of determination that I've never seen on her before. Kind of like she's been starving on a desert island and has just laid her eyes on an angry (but juicy) wild boar.

When the music begins, her hips start swaying to the beat like her life depends on it. And suddenly I have no doubt this is someone living their dream. Because she takes a boring church song—and she rocks it.

After the show's over, we give Sadie hugs and high fives, and then Mo and his parents go with her to get her stuff, and my mom and I head out to the parking lot. Lots of people are still standing around talking. And then I spot Miranda and her dad.

"Mom," I say. "Can we go congratulate Miranda?"

"Sure," she says. "She was great."

"Yeah, but I'm pretty sure her dad isn't going to be happy about her performance."

My mom eyes him, looks down at her jeans, and takes a deep breath. "Then we should support her however we can."

We walk over together, and as soon as we get close, I say, "Miranda, you were wonderful!"

"You really were," my mom agrees.

Miranda nods, but she doesn't smile. She glances at her dad.

"That is not how I saw it," Rick Adams snaps. "There's nothing wonderful about such unladylike dancing." He turns to my mom. "Eliza, as a parent, I would expect you to agree."

"I—" My mom's voice falters for a moment, but then she continues. "I don't think there was anything unladylike about Miranda's performance. I saw a young woman bringing a song to life beautifully."

Is my mom actually arguing with Rick Adams?

"Did you hear the applause, Mr. Adams?" I add. "There was a huge crowd that thought she was wonderful."

Mr. Adams's jaw is set. He turns to leave. "Well, this is not up for public discussion. I'm her father, and she will—"

"Think for myself," Miranda cuts in.

He looks back. "What did you just say?"

Miranda's voice is shaking, but her jaw is as firm as her dad's. "I'll think for myself."

"Miranda—"

But she doesn't let him finish. "You had no right to read my diary."

153

Mr. Adams's eyes flash. "We are not having this conversation here."

"You won't even deny it," Miranda says loud enough for people to start looking over.

In the crowd, I spot Tya with her family, and I catch her eye.

Her dad's voice drops to a whisper. "We are in public."

"I know," Miranda says, not whispering at all. "Put your best foot forward in public. That's what you always say." She looks around. Even more people are starting to stare. "But what about putting the truth forward? When's that supposed to happen?"

At that moment, Tya appears on one side of Miranda and then Jaclyn appears on the other. "You know, that's a good question," Jaclyn says. "And Pastor Paul has told us it's really good to ask questions."

Tya puts her arm around Miranda. "What was that Pastor Paul said at the end of class this week? That if God lives inside each of us, one of the best ways to love God is to love ourselves? I'd say that performance was a whole truckload of loving God."

Mr. Adams's lips press into a thin line. "Miranda, it's time for dinner."

Miranda ignores her dad and turns to the three of us, her eyes bright. "It sure felt like that." She looks back at her dad. "You can have dinner without me tonight, and I don't need a ride home either. I'll walk."

His eyes shift. Is that sadness creeping in? "Fine," he says quietly. "Use that time to think."

As we watch her dad head for his car, Miranda lets out a huge breath. "I can't believe I just did that."

"You did great," I say. "It might have been even more impressive than your fabulous performance onstage."

"Are you going to be all right going home?" my mom asks. "Does your dad . . ." She pauses. "Ever get too angry with you?"

Miranda shakes her head. "He might send me to my room to pray, but I can handle that." She smiles. "I've got a lot of praying to do anyway to thank God for the courage He gave me."

Tya gives Miranda a squeeze. "Before you go home . . . my family's taking me out for dinner. You want to come with us?"

"I'd love that," Miranda says.

"We're getting pie, too, of course," Tya says, grinning.

Miranda grins back. "Well, you're the one who should get to eat one hundred and fifty pieces of pie all by herself. I'll just try to keep up."

Chapter 44

MY MOM'S BOOK OF POEMS BY RUMI HAS A LINE I LOVE. *Set your life on fire. Seek those who fan your flames.* I can't stop thinking about it, and about Gracy. And how lucky I am to live on her street, and that she volunteered to take me to my orthodontist.

I decide I want to make her something. So I spend some time with my mom's markers, practicing script and tiny designs and then looking for just the right phrase in just the right poem . . . until I realize I already know what I want to write.

On Saturday morning the gift is ready, so I text Gracy: Can I come over? I have something for you.

Gracy texts back right away: Perfect timing! And I have something I think you'll be interested in seeing. Come right on over!

When Gracy comes to the door, I present her with a decorated to-go container. "For your anthropology club dinners."

Gracy lets out a huge hoot of laughter. "Girl, you *get* me." She runs her fingers along the words, *her* words, written around the rim. *It just takes enough of them finding a way, and then they've reshaped the future.*

"I'm so glad those words stayed with you." Gracy says. Then she gives me a squeeze. "Do you want to come around back?"

Gracy leads me to the old picnic table.

It's covered with skulls.

"Wow." I breathe as I take in each one laid out in the sunshine.

Gracy picks a skull up and examines it. "I always love the way it's possible to see things in a new way once you strip something down to its bones."

My fingers trace the curves of the other skulls. "It's cool how they're all different shapes and sizes."

Gracy nods. "There's a wide range of ways to exist in this world."

I pause when I get to the opossum skull. "When you told me about that first written poem, about how they imagined God as a She . . . that opened something inside me. Like I was a sealed box before, just trying to stay small and closed up tight." I swallow. "But once you realize you can open up, you can't go back. Because you realize there's so much you don't want to miss." I look at Gracy. "Thank you."

Gracy puts her arm around me. "It's been a beautiful thing to witness."

Her arm around me feels so warm and strong. "I started imagining God as looking like Maya Angelou," I say. "And then

I realized I didn't even have to stop there. That God can be even bigger, even wider."

"When it's your imagining, you never have to stop," Gracy says. "Maya Angelou. Malala Yousafzai. Frida Kahlo. People who loved themselves and believed in themselves and put that goodness into the world. Each one expands our understanding of a higher power."

I smile at her. "You do that, too."

Gracy puts her hand on my shoulder. "You know, when I think of God, I imagine an enormous, invisible fabric connecting everyone, the threads weaving through each one of us. Because we *all* can live like that. Like we've got a higher power flowing inside us."

I touch the opossum's teeth. "Even if we're still figuring things out?"

"Especially then," she says. "You know, I'm pretty sure asking questions is its own kind of higher power. Right up there with telling the truth."

I feel the sunlight all around me. As bright as headlights. As powerful as the force of love.

It's on us to not freeze up.

To keep our eyes wide open.

— *Chapter 45* —

ON SUNDAY AFTERNOON I TEXT MO. YOU FREE?

Yep.

Want to write?

Together?

Yeah.

You bet! Your house or mine?

What if we meet back at the sheep pen?

You sure? **he types.**

Most def. It's oozing stories.

Deal.

An hour later, Mo leans his bike against one side of the sheep pen. "I have to tell you something before we get started."

I drop my bag on the ground. "What?"

"It doesn't matter that my shopping cart story didn't win the contest." He starts hopping from one foot to the other, looking like he's going to burst. "Because the president of the high school literary magazine was one of the judges, and he wrote to me! And told me it was 'original!' And 'out of the box!' AND he wants me to start submitting material to the magazine! And to be on staff as soon as we're in high school!"

"That's amazing!" I pull him into a hug. "And what a way to get your parents off your back," I say, grinning. "Literary magazine contributor. That resume will write itself."

"I told him about you, too, and he said you should submit stuff too if you want."

I eye my notebook of opossum entries. "I'll think about it." But my grin only gets bigger.

"So what are you thinking of writing today?" he says as he takes out his notebook. "Do you want to write more opossum entries? And I can start a new shopping cart story."

"I'm ready to write something together again."

His eyes light up. "Really? Write like we used to?"

"No," I say, still grinning. "Because we're way better writers than before. Our next story will be even more amazing."

"Yes!" Mo pumps his fist. "Because we're even more amazing."

"Yeah, and that's the thing with stories, right?" I say. "A lot depends on who's telling it."

Mo flips open his notebook. "Okay, so where should it start? And who are the characters? In the sheep pen or . . . no, no sheep pen. No sheep for this story."

I walk the length of the sheep pen. "Maybe there are sheep, but they refuse to stay in the pen. They smash into the wall until it falls apart and then leap over the rubble and run through the long grass together." I hold up my finger. "And the grass is safe because the ticks have been eaten by the giant opossum that lives up the hill."

"Oh yes, I can picture it," says Mo, scribbling in his notebook. "I think the field should have some monuments in the distance, like a nod to the authors." He keeps writing. "One will say: Mo: Who Discovered New Ways to Know Things, and the other will say: Agnes!" He looks up. "Have you been thinking about what you want your monument to say?"

I look out into the field where I can picture the monuments just like he can. I think for a few minutes, and when I have it, I announce: "Agnes: Who Realized She Could Tell Her Own Story."

"That's perfect," Mo says.

I sit down next to him and watch as he writes it all down. "There should be some shopping carts, too, right?" I say.

"Oh yes!" He pulls his backpack over and starts digging inside. "Hey, we need some brain food. My mom packed us some sliced apples."

He holds out the baggie and I take a thin slice. "You know, opossums love apples, too," I tell him.

"They have good taste," he says. "I'm forming a good opinion about them, Agnes. Not that they care. Maybe they wouldn't be so angry if they had more apples."

"You're funny, Mo. And I'm pretty sure opossums can find plenty of apples on their own." I hold the apple slice between my fingers. "I think what they want is to simply be allowed to eat their apples in peace."

Mo crunches through his apple slice. "That shouldn't be too much to ask."

"No, it shouldn't."

I turn to a new page in my notebook as I bite into an apple slice and savor the sweet, invigorating taste. Together, we start to write . . .

Once there were sheep, crammed together in a too-small pen. But they were big sheep with big ideas, and they decided they weren't willing to stay stuck inside those stone walls any longer.

"Maybe they should stack themselves on top of each other to escape," Mo says.

I nod. "Or they could become like battering rams. Sheepish battering rams."

"And then they can argue about the best way to get out."

I jot it all down and grin. "It turns out our sheep aren't very sheeplike after all."

As the big sheep were arguing, the smallest one in the corner started poking at a rock in the wall . . . until it came

loose and rolled onto the ground. So she started poking at
another . . .

Acknowledgments

I WILL ALWAYS REMEMBER (AND WILL BE FOREVER grateful for!) the moment the idea for this book sparked into place. I was out to dinner with some wonderful librarians in Virginia in 2019 when Lara Ivey turned to me and said, possibly joking but possibly not: "For your next book . . . how about an opossum?"

The fact that the many layers of an opossum fit so perfectly into the story that was already taking shape in my head speaks to the innate brilliance of Lara and to the innate brilliance of the universe itself.

There was another moment, decades earlier, that I'll also always be grateful for. I had been an active member of the youth group at my church and loved it. We ate, did service projects, and laughed, and our associate pastor, Rev. David Spollett, made hymn singing extra fun by dancing to the beat. And then at some point we had elections, and the newly elected youth president made a new rule: We should all sign a form saying that we believed in God. The problem was that as much as I loved church, I just wasn't there yet. I wanted to believe, but every time I saw an image of God as an old (and maybe angry) man with a long white beard, it stopped me short.

I really loved Reverend Spollett, and I talked to him about it. He encouraged me to push back against this whole idea of signing a pledge. Since I didn't have the confidence to do that, I dropped out of youth group. But I was still a member of the church, and Reverend Spollett invited me to be a youth member on our church's search committee for a new pastor. Suddenly, I was reading potential candidates' statements of faith and being exposed to some of the many wide-ranging ways people can define God for themselves: As the thread that connects us. As hope. As love. And with that, a whole world of faith opened up for me. So thank you, Rev. David Spollett, for the unconditional love you gave to me and my questions, and for the wide-open air of possibility with which you surrounded us.

I am also thankful to the folks working to expand our view of history so that it's about all people, not just men—and so appreciative of the books that broadened my viewpoint, including *Who Cooked the Last Supper? The Women's History of the World* by Rosalind Miles; *The Invisible Sex: Uncovering the True Roles of Women in Prehistory* by J. M. Adovasio, Olga Soffer, and Jake Page; *Women's Work: The First 20,000 Years* by Elizabeth Wayland Barber; *From Eve to Dawn: A History of Women in the World* (volume I) by Marilyn French; and several books and essays by Karen Armstrong, in particular *In the Beginning: A New Interpretation of Genesis* and *A History of God*.

And of course, I'm thankful for Maya Angelou, who showed us all the power of putting one's own personal truth out into the world—and onto the page.

Like many books, this particular book was shaped by people who took time out of their lives to help make it better: Janae Marks for reading an early version of this manuscript and knowing exactly what revisions were needed; Karen Avery (Sparky) who was part of the inspiration behind Gracy and who taught me how her relationship with roadkill changed once she had a skull collection; Colleen the Opossum Queen for answering my opossum questions; and Michael Clough and the Southern Vermont Natural History Museum who let me meet (and name!) Momo the Opossum.

I'd have never been able to finish a first draft or know how to rewrite it—or be able to finish that rewrite or complete the many revisions after that—if it hadn't been for my critique group the Rocket Cats (otherwise known as Elaine Vickers, Jennifer Chambliss Bertman, and Tara Dairman). With brilliant insight and unwavering encouragement, the four of us formed a FOOT group before any FOOT group existed on the page. You are the ones who fan the flames of my writing fire, and I will always be grateful.

To my agent, Tricia Lawrence, my fairy godmother, Kirsten Cappy, and the whole team at Erin Murphy Literary Agency: I couldn't have written a story like this without knowing there were people like you in my corner, supporting me at every turn.

Thank you also to the entire team at Nancy Paulsen Books and Penguin Random House who helped guide this book along its path, especially cover artist Chanelle Nibbelink, whose gorgeous re-creation of Agnes's brain—and smirk!—makes me smile every time I see it; cover designer Jessica Jenkins; associate publishing manager Sara LaFleur; copyeditors Ariela Rudy Zaltzman and Michelle Lippold; my publicist, Lizzie Goodell; and Trevor Ingerson and the entire fabulous team at Penguin Classroom.

To my editor Nancy Paulsen, who not only DIDN'T run away when I said "What about a dead opossum? And questions about religion? And shopping carts?" but who also had the infinite wisdom needed to turn my wild ideas into a beautifully shaped (and still wild) story: Thank you for having the vision to make this book what it is. I don't know many people who better epitomize what is looks like to have waves of a higher power coursing through them. I'm honored to be in your sphere of influence.

When you have written a story as personal as this one, the core of your gratitude belongs with the people who have shaped you as a person the most.

To my mom, who raised me by herself and was always ready—in her own quiet way—to support me being who I was, instead of who others wanted me to be. What wasn't quiet: the two of us belting out "Joy to the World" in the car on every Christmas Day as we replaced all the *hes* with *shes*. (Plus, there's nothing like finding out that your mom, who you saw as quite the rule follower, refused to memorize the Apostles' Creed for her confirmation class because she didn't think she should have to memorize what she believed.)

To my best friend, Amy, who once split an all-butter coffee cake down the middle with me and was by my side from first grade on as we spent our days playing double solitaire (Nerts!) and laughing over bizarre jokes no one else was ever going to understand.

To my daughter, Alice, who at seven years old helped me write some of Sadie's lines and who still has that confidence— and who I hope will never lose it.

To Ethan, for giving me the privilege to live with the deep, questioning, and powerful mind of a twelve-year-old. I am so lucky to be your mom.

And above all, for my husband, Dan. When you begin a relationship by personifying abandoned shopping carts together, you know you've found the best teammate there could be. And when you catch him replacing of the *he* pronouns with *she* when reading *Winnie-the-Pooh* aloud (and is even more outraged than you are about how out of balance the original was), you know you've found the best co-parent as well. Thank you for cheering me—and this story—on every step of the way.

Then they rode off into the sunset, two shopping carts who, together, could be fully themselves—and who knew how beautifully free and wonderful that felt . . .